A
Garden
TO DIE FOR
The Coffee House Sleuths

A Garden

TO DIE FOR

The Coffee House Sleuths

T. LOCKHAVEN

EDITED BY:
EMMY ELLIS
GRACE LOCKHAVEN

TWISTED KEY
p u b l i s h i n g

2020

First Printing: 2020

ISBN 978-1-947744-46-2

Twisted Key Publishing, LLC
www.twistedkeypublishing.com

Ordering Information:
Special discounts are available on quantity purchases by corporations, associations, educators, and others. For details, contact the publisher at the above listed address.

U.S. trade bookstores and wholesalers: Please contact Twisted Key Publishing, LLC by email twistedkeypublishing@gmail.com.

Contents

Chapter 1

The Bitter Sweet Café

Lana Cove, North Carolina, June

Michael West checked his rearview mirror for cops. Satisfied, he edged his shiny red Miata to the center of the two-lane highway, eating the tiny dotted white lines with his car as if playing Pac-Man. It was the simple things in life that amused him.

The sky was beautiful. Thin wispy clouds stretched taffy-like across a cerulean canvas. The warm, morning sunlight made Michael think of fresh apple pie. His thick brown hair danced playfully as he raced along, the ocean glistening to his left, sand dunes and seagrass to his right. It was a perfect spring day.

One hundred forty-two, Michael concluded. That was the number of white lines he'd successfully consumed on his drive, a new record. He nosed his car into the parking lot behind the Bitter Sweet Café. For many years, this had been home of the Bait and Hook Tackle Shop, a family-owned business, but after fifty years, the Meyers decided to call it quits and put it up for sale.

Ellie Banks and Olivia, family friends, had purchased the building from the Meyers and now ran the café. After months of planning and renovations, the Bitter Sweet Café was finally ready. The architecture was a beautiful mixture of coquina stone and caramel stucco. If you were a chocolate aficionado (a.k.a. chocolate snob), you would instantly deduce that the architecture was inspired by a Milky Way bar—chocolate-colored roof and trimmings, the outer walls, a rich and caramel.

Attached to the front was a large wooden deck that extended out to the boardwalk. Ellie and Olivia had spent many sleepless nights trying to decide whether they should keep the original deck, the wood grayed and stooped like an old man, and romantic sentiments were carved into the woodwork: Tyler and Jane. Forty-two years later, Tyler and Jane sat at that very bench every Tuesday for lunch.

In the end, they decided to keep the original deck as a homage to the past owners and locals. Besides, Tyler and Jane were too adorable—the deck would just have to remain there until they died, which didn't appear to be any time soon.

Michael reached over to the passenger seat and unbelted his notepad. To the casual observer, it was a plain, well-used, run-of-the-mill, blue-lined, college-ruled notepad, but to Michael, it was where he had poured his heart and soul over the past three months. It was his soon-to-be-published detective thriller, *Killer Canvas*.

His friends had commented on the scribbles and cross-outs on his notepad and insisted that a laptop would be easier. But for Michael, creativity was never something that should be easy, it should be crafted, refined, worked and reworked. He liked the sound, the feeling of pencil on paper—it felt raw, scratchy, like it was a part of his own being, transferred to the page.

He climbed out of his Miata, pushed the door closed with his hip, and then out of habit, locked the doors of his convertible over his shoulder. *Chirp. Chirp.*

He slid his tortoiseshell Ray-Bans atop his head and strode inside the Bitter Sweet Café. A soft melodic jingle announced his arrival. Michael breathed in deeply, filling his lungs with the rich aroma of freshly baked bread and heavenly coffee. Light, ethereal jazz filled the air. If he had any worries, the moment he stepped through the doorway, they simply vaporized. The Bitter Sweet Café had that *it* factor, the type of atmosphere that appealed to all walks of life; everyone fit in there. Like the multitude of colors on an artist's palette, clumps of locals were gathered throughout, immersed in their own little worlds, deep in conversation.

Michael's gaze quickly slid across the room; the familiar groups were all there. The realtors, dressed in their fine linen suits and colorful silk ties, commandeered a group of tables near the front entrance, waiting to pick off any unfortunate tourist who meandered close enough to get caught up in their gravitational pull.

Michael smiled at Terry, a man with a toupee that no longer matched his silver eyebrows and sideburns. He'd been disappointed to learn that Michael had already purchased a house in Lana Cove. Michael had drawn a chorus of hisses from Terry's comrades when he'd said he'd bought the house from real-estate mogul, Maxwell King, the self-professed king of real estate.

The tennis club, dressed in pastels and whites, was seated by the floor-to-ceiling window, facing the deck, the occupants enjoying golden-brown crepes and wild berry spritzers.

And then there were the seniors. Oh…the seniors were a rowdy bunch. They were the troublemakers. Every morning, they pushed the tables at the back of the café together, creating one ominous table that extended across the entirety of the wall. There wasn't enough room for another chair. Michael figured one or two of them would have to die soon, or they were simply going to have to expand the width of the café.

Michael was quite sure that this seating arrangement was the inspiration for Leonardo's *Last Supper* painting. The occupants, with their oversized floppy sun hats and awkwardly long shorts and crisp white sneakers, certainly looked old enough to have been around when he walked the earth. Unfortunately, in this scenario, Arthur Wisley, an eighty-year-old burlesque dancer on the weekends (allegedly), was a would-be Jesus.

Michael let his imagination go there for a moment, shook his head, and then searched the lengthy silver-and-glass countertop that extended along the front wall for Ellie, the barista and half-owner of the Bitter Sweet Café.

He found her crouched below the counter, placing a fresh pan of muffins into the glass display. Her brown ponytail had fallen forward over her shoulder. It was either trying to help her or it simply enjoyed muffins.

"Good morning, Michael," she called up, straightening the muffins into perfect rows of delectable debauchery, then with a deft flick of the hand, sent her ponytail back behind her.

Michael imagined a sharp, surprised cry emanating from her ponytail: "Ah!"

"Morning, Ellie. The muffins look delicious. How are you?"

"Wonderful." She brushed her hands on her apron, a dazzling smile spreading.

The door jingled behind Michael as another customer came into the café. A woman's voice chirped, finishing up her phone call.

"I like the shirt." Ellie gestured toward Michael's red, Hawaiian-inspired, short-sleeved shirt, tastefully adorned with large white flowers and green parrots.

"Thanks." Michael smiled and studied her carefully to see if she was teasing him or being honest. "It helps me get into the mood to write, you know," he explained, "by embracing the look and feel of my main protagonist."

Ellie nodded and flicked some stray crumbs off the countertop into her hand. "Isn't your main protagonist in Italy? Or, wait, was he born in Hawaii and moved to Italy? Or maybe, he was born in Italy but wants to move to Hawaii!"

"You're funny. He's at the airport, about to fly to Italy." He narrowed his eyes. "What do you think? It's a little too *Magnum PI*-ish? I want to be original."

"Oh no." Ellie shook her head. "That shirt is *definitely* you. Besides, you don't have enough chest hair to pull off the *Magnum*."

Michael couldn't decide if that was an insult or simply a valid point. He immediately cursed his decision to use the laser hair removal coupon he'd found on Groupon. "I always thought his chest was a little…," he paused to emphasize his point, "too hairy. Deforestation comes to mind."

"Is that what you think?" Ellie smiled.

"Yes," Michael said indignantly. "Magnum was shallow and all about sex appeal and shiny sports cars. I strive to create in-depth characters, people you feel you could be friends with…relate to."

"Mhm." Ellie dropped the crumbs into the trashcan. "I see, says the man who drives a red convertible." She waited a moment to let her little jab soak in. "So, the usual? Hazelnut, skim milk, a pinch of cinnamon, and a *half* a teaspoon of sugar."

Michael bristled as the woman behind him snickered. He leaned onto the counter and whispered, "Ellie, must you announce *all* of the ingredients?"

Ellie placed her hands on the counter, mirroring him. "Yes," she whispered loudly.

"Isn't that some breach of the coffee confidentiality bylaws—perhaps the coffee ethics statute or something?"

"I don't believe so, Michael, but…," she gently placed her hand on his, leaning in closer, "I *do* respect a man who possesses such forbearance. *Any* other man would have splurged and asked for an *entire* teaspoon of sugar, maybe…even two."

"Or whole milk, maybe even…*cream*," the woman behind him added, exaggerating the word cream.

"Exactly, Gail." Ellie nodded approvingly, waving a spoon her way. "But not you, mister. I say be proud of who you are."

"You scoff, but I'll have you know, that this physique"—he paused and waved his hand up and down his torso—"was forged through abstinence." He immediately regretted his word choice and held up a finger, requesting what is known in the world of pontification, and golf, as a do-over. "This fortress of manhood was sculpted through *denial*…," his voice tapered off.

"Denial?" Gail asked, giggling.

"It's a *large* river in Egypt," Ellie snickered.

"Well," Gail said, playfully, "if you ever find yourself in *denial,* without a paddle…here's my card."

Ellie snorted. "Michael, meet Gail Bradley," she said, affection in her tone. "She's the owner of—"

"CyanScentific Marketing, off of Sea Grape Avenue," Gail interrupted. "Sorry El." She wrinkled her nose. "I just like saying it. CyanScentific. I love the way it just rolls off the tongue."

"Oh, yes, I've seen it." Michael nodded. "The *lilac*-colored building, right…? *Very* tasteful. Wasn't that building Gary's funeral home?"

"We don't speak of such things," Ellie whispered and held a finger to her lips. "Gail's offended by death; she finds it intrusive."

"Actually, periwinkle," Gail corrected.

"You're offended by periwinkle?" Michael asked.

"No, the color of my building is periwinkle, not lilac."

"My apologies, I'm a bit of a color neophyte."

Gail waved aside his ignorance of colors and continued. "So, anyways, my business card, it's scented with lavender."

"Lavender helps with stress and relaxation," Ellie explained.

"Interesting. So...." Michael paused, reading. "Cryosentific Marketing? Isn't that where you freeze people?"

"Funny." Gail smiled. "No, darling, what you are referring to is cryogenics, where you can freeze things for a long period of time and then revive them...kind of like that shirt you're wearing."

Ellie snorted and then pretended to wipe down the counter.

"The name *CyanScentific* comes from the blending of aromatherapy and color therapy. Cyan, for the color, and Scent for the aromatherapy. I make business cards, scented candles, air fresheners, and stationary supplies for companies by combining those components.

"For example," Gail continued. "Blue is especially popular with financial institutions because it inspires trust. I lightly scent their business cards and candles with lavender because, according to the cognitive psychology unit at Leiden Institute for brain cognition, lavender inspires trust."

"What do you think? Brilliant, right? Michael was a big-time advertising executive in Boston," Ellie explained to Gail. "Now he's just unemployed." She winked.

"I love the idea. It's very clever, a very niche concept," Michael said.

"An advertising expert." Gail placed her hand on Michael's shoulder.

However, to Michael it felt more like a fishhook, and he was about to be reeled in.

Gail went on, "If you're not too busy, maybe you and I could—"

Michael glanced at his watch and gave her a disappointed look. "I'm sorry…Gail." He nodded toward the café deck. "I've got to get to work. My editor," he shook his head, "she's given me an impossible deadline." He turned, grabbed his coffee from the counter, and slipped a sleeve over the paper cup.

"Maybe some other time," Gail insisted.

"Yes, yes, definitely, some other time."

"Well, you've got my card, you know how to reach me."

"Of course, yes." He paused. "Gail, lovely to meet you. Thank you for the business card and the science lesson." He retrieved his notebook from the counter. "Ellie…." He smiled broadly. "It's *always* a pleasure."

"Enjoy writing. It's a beautiful day out there." Ellie beamed and gestured toward the deck.

"Thank you, I will." He waved.

"He's a hot mess." Gail laughed, watching Michael as he strolled across the café, out the door, and into the dazzling sunlight.

Chapter 2

The Writer in Me

The Bitter Sweet Café's deck had its own *unique* feel. While the coffee shop proper was chic and classy, the weatherworn, splinter-filled deck looked like it had been in a fight with a hurricane and lost...twice. The décor consisted of two rows of circular wooden tables and goliath-sized matching chairs that required at least two months at the local cross-fit gym to be able to move them.

Michael maneuvered through the tables, to his favorite spot located at the back corner of the deck. This was his safe haven, the place where magic happened. He felt somewhat secluded, tucked away in the corner, but was still very much a part of everything going on around him. From his vantage point was a view of the boardwalk, the ocean, and he could subtly spy on—or rather, observe—the café patrons, *for character studies*, without appearing creepy.

Michael placed his coffee on his table and straddled the back of the gargantuan deck chair. He must resemble a sumo wrestler about to do battle. He grabbed the back of the chair and heaved, scraping the legs of the enormous beast across the wooden floorboards, fingernails on a chalkboard.

When he'd first arrived in Lana Cove in March, he'd apologized every time he moved a chair, trying desperately not to annoy fellow patrons with the loud grating sound. He recalled his first awkward experience when he'd attempted to joke with the locals about the weight of the chairs.

"Who needs a gym?" Michael had asked. "Just come here and rearrange the chairs. Am I right?"

Crickets.... The diners simply stared at him with what could only be described as pitied annoyance.

But then again, the chess club probably wasn't the optimal audience for his sophisticated sense of humor. Michael, however, was not one to simply surrender. He regrouped and tried again the next day.

"Seems they found the furniture from the Titanic," Michael said, leaning on the back of a chair. "No wonder it sank! ...Aww, come on, nothing? Too soon?" he asked a table of colorfully dressed octogenarians, appearing entirely like a basket of freshly dyed Easter eggs.

No sooner had the words *too soon* escaped his lips than a petite woman stepped outside, ushering a cluster of tourists to a table. Expertly balancing a tray filled with water glasses in one hand, she effortlessly slid the massive chairs from beneath the table with her free hand, without spilling a drop.

If the utter, complete annihilation of his own masculinity wasn't bad enough, a bald, bewhiskered man, with saggy jowls, scoffed at him, pursed his moist lips, and made a raspberry sound directed at Michael, whilst his friends gawped on, shaking their heads in bitter disappointment. Michael had later learned that this group of seniors was the *anti-bullying committee* for the town of Lana Cove.

Feeling the need to reconnect with his manhood, that evening, Michael went home, burned his *Yoga-Lite* DVDs and cancelled his subscription to *Horse Fancy* magazine.

Eventually, after three months in Lana Cove, the locals had begrudgingly begun to accept Michael as one of their own. He'd checked all of the boxes required to be a local. He'd bought a house; he wasn't renting. He'd purchased lawn ornaments. He was taking piano lessons from Elizabeth Archer, and, most importantly, Ellie seemed to have befriended him, and if Ellie had taken a liking to him, well, he couldn't be all bad.

Michael yawned and took a much-anticipated sip of coffee and settled back into his chair, having returned to the present. The warmth of the sunbaked wood against his back and forearms felt heavenly. He breathed the salty ocean air deep into his lungs, letting it slowly escape. He could have easily fallen asleep right there.

He reached for his coffee and then laughed. Ellie had penciled in his name as *Adonis*—the god of beauty—on the side of his cup.

Ellie.... He turned and tried to peer into the café window, hoping to catch a glimpse of her, but the sun beat on the glass, and all he could make out was a forty-year-old man with wavy brown hair and an obnoxious red shirt staring back at him.

For a moment, Michael felt foolish, a forty-year-old divorcee who'd walked out of his job in Boston, at the top of his game. The familiar weight of doubt crawled up his spine, its hands heavy on his shoulders, creeping up his neck to his brain.

"No," he whispered, shaking his head. "No, we're not going down that rabbit hole again. This is your new life, a new beginning, embrace it." He exhaled and nodded as if he'd received a *you can do it* pep talk from a good friend.

Ellie passed by the window. She paused and made a *tap-tap* sound with her fingernail on the glass. She smiled and pointed to his notebook, and then gestured that he should be writing.

Michael's face flushed. It was as if she knew he was thinking about her. He watched her as she turned and walked away, disappearing into the glaring reflection of the glass, until only his reflection remained.

To him, Ellie was an enigma, like the ocean—you could walk along her shores and pick up the little treasures she left along the way. You could wade in the shallows, but try to go in too deep, and you'd face a barrage of waves that would relentlessly push you back to the shore.

Michael had learned not to ask the locals about her, so he didn't know much about her personal life. He knew she was single and divorced, but that was about it. In Lana Cove they respected privacy, and if Ellie wanted to tell you something, she'd tell you. So for now, Michael found himself wading in the shallows, wondering if Ellie would ever let him past the breakers.

A gust of wind blew, flipping back the pages of his notebook. He smiled looking at the sketches he'd drawn over the past three months of people he'd observed on the deck. He had a page dedicated to heads—egg-shaped, round, oblong, protruding brows, collapsed jawlines, each with a caption beneath them.

Another page he dedicated to unique voices and accents. Another was titled Idiosyncrasies of Human Behavior. The Bitter Sweet Café deck was a wonderful place to study people of all shapes, sizes, and ages, from all over the world.

One woman, a local, always arrived alone. She sat, hung her purse on the side of her chair, and then aligned her utensils and the salt and pepper shakers in perfect rows. She'd then take the napkin from the table, fold it twice, place it across her legs, and wait with her hands clasped in her lap until a server appeared. She had a wedding band on her left-hand ring finger, but Michael never saw her with anyone. She never read, never checked her phone, she just quietly ate, occasionally letting her eyes take in the occupants of the deck.

This was one of the complexities of public decorum. She must be incredibly lonely, but then again, that was his interpretation. She obviously needed a routine, but was she happy? Was she content sitting alone day after day? Maybe this was her form of meditation. Maybe she had an exceptionally busy life or challenging job, and this was her moment of solace. He really didn't know anything about her. Michael jotted a few thoughts into his notepad. Another's happiness, to others, may look sorrowful or tragic. Michael hoped that it was this daily ceremony that brought her happiness.

One of the sweetest things he had observed was older couples tended to wear clothes that complemented the other person's attire. A couple would arrive, he in khaki Bermuda shorts with a matching white knit shirt, she in a khaki skirt and a white top. They even accessorized the same. He might have a green hat, and she had a beautiful ivy-green purse. He wondered if this was intentional, or if after long periods of time, people unconsciously melded into a single person. Sure, they may have different thoughts, but all of their actions were the same. They ate the same foods, watched the same shows, listened to the same music, used the same toothpaste. They occupied different bodies...but had they basically become the same person?

Younger couples didn't bother to match; they hardly even acknowledged each other. They'd quickly glance at the menu, pull out their phones and earbuds, completely disappearing into whatever happened to be taking place on their screen.

Michael used to worry that conversation was going to become a lost art form conveyed in a series of emojis. But then seniors exhibited the same behavior. Only, instead of disappearing into a tiny screen, they completely hid themselves from their partners behind kite-sized newspaper pages, shaking their heads and muttering aloud to themselves.

So, Michael concluded that in reality, not much had changed. Whether a screen or a newspaper, people would always find a way to ignore the person sitting across from them. One thing he knew for certain was that if you simply paid attention, the world would write the stories for you…you simply had to want to be a part of it all.

Michael flipped through his notepad, taking a few minutes to reread the last two pages he'd written. He scribbled some notes along the edge of the page, made a few corrections, and then he wrote in earnest. The story flowed through his imagination like a dream. It was three hours later when a woman's high-pitched laughter tickled his consciousness and drew him from his writing.

He glanced up. A petite woman, her hair pulled back in a ponytail, a smile on her face, enjoyed the company of her friends. Michael grinned to himself, raised his hands above his head, and stretched his shoulders. The deck was brimming with activity— the lunch crowd had arrived.

"Hey, you," a singsong voice said. "You were writing, so I didn't want to bother you."

"Good morn...afternoon, Olivia," Michael corrected himself, checking his watch. "How are you?"

"Great! So...." She placed a hand on his table, leaning in. "Ellie and I got a bunch of hungry mouths to feed. Give me a quick synopsis of where we are in the story."

Michael smiled again. He had basically written his entire novel sitting in the café and out here on the deck. Olivia, the co-owner of the café, acted as his sounding board, letting him know if he was straying from his outline. She was the rudder of his tiny vessel.

"Okay, here's where we left off." He flipped through his notes. "So, the thieves have hidden in the Santa Maria Maddalena church in Italy. Their target, the *Crucifixion,* a painting worth over three million dollars," he explained.

"All right." Olivia nodded. "So, they've figured out how to get in without tripping alarms and being seen."

"Yes, they attended mass, you know, as ordinary parishioners. Just as it was about to end, they slipped out of the sanctuary, disappeared into a restroom, and climbed up into the ceiling."

"I'm confused." Olivia knotted her eyebrows. "You said that the police were tipped off that the painting was going to be stolen, and the original was moved to a secure location. Why are they still continuing with the robbery?"

"Yes, yes, it's part of the thieves' plan, part of the distraction. The thieves wanted the painting to be moved to another location."

Olivia looked at Michael wearily. "I feel like you are leaving out some important details."

"Maybe." Michael grinned. "I could tell you more but—"

"No," Olivia interrupted, "I want to be surprised. There's nothing better than a good twist in a story." She beamed brightly at Michael, her blue eyes even bluer beneath the cloudless sky.

"I'll do my best. If this baby's not a success," he tapped the notepad for emphasis, "I'm gonna be out there on the beach," Michael gestured toward the shoreline, "swinging a metal detector like those old guys."

"Oh…not so sure you want to do that. You already lost a round to the anti-bullying seniors' group. I hear the beachcombers don't take too kindly to newbies encroaching on their turf."

"They're like eighty years old. Look at them. They carry tiny plastic shovels in their belts."

Olivia shook her head, crossing her arms. "I hear that Mr. Wimbly tried to move in on their territory…," she paused, drawing her lips together tightly.

"What, they kicked sand in his face? Stole his dentures?"

"Worse," Olivia said darkly. "They trampled his flower garden and stole his welcome mat."

"Okay, that is excessive, no one deserves that."

"Michael, think twice before you do anything rash. With those big squishy tires and their recumbent bikes, you'll never hear them coming."

"Thank you, Olivia. Good advice, good advice."

"All right." Olivia took a quick look over her shoulder. "I've ignored my guests long enough. Are you staying for lunch?"

"I wish I could." Michael glanced at his watch. "I've actually got a massive kudzu infestation threatening to devour my fence and weeping willow. My afternoon involves me, a shovel, and the finest boxed wine money can buy." He arched his eyebrows enticingly. "Interested?"

"Kudzu…infestation? You may want to see a doctor about that." Olivia winked. "You don't want those things to overpopulate."

"Yeah," Michael said. "I may have to contact *plant-parenthood*."

"Oh, Michael, and you wonder why you're still single." Olivia laughed and walked away.

"Who says I'm single?" Michael called out.

"Your shirt," she yelled back over her shoulder. "Your shirt says it all."

Chapter 3

Herb Problem

Michael stood on his back porch eyeing the large twisty vines that had completely covered his white picket fence and were now strangling his prized weeping willow. "Kudzu," he spat.

Michael had just returned home after spending an hour at Rosemary's Garden, learning everything he could about kudzu annihilation. Two hundred and seventy dollars later, and a head filled with plant-killing knowledge, Michael felt completely prepared to defeat the invasive plant—organically and humanely, by hacking and chopping it into pieces with a razor-sharp machete and a titanium-tipped shovel.

Having lived in Boston Proper his entire life, Michael hadn't really done any gardening, or murdered any plants, unless you included his Earth Science class, where he soaked a lima bean on a wet paper towel. He remembered the fragile root system, green and coiled, so delicate, so soft, so susceptible to an uninterrupted heat source provided by an infrared lamp—mistakenly left on over the entire weekend.

Not being one to give up, Michael later used the scorched lima bean example at the science fair, where he did a presentation on skin cancer. *How to Know When You've Bean in the Sun Too Long*. How difficult could it be to remove some kudzu?

Per Rosemary's expert advice, Michael set up a staging area on his back porch. He'd purchased steel-toed, corn-yellow work boots (in case he missed with his titanium-tipped shovel or machete) and a wide-brimmed hat to protect him from the sun.

Michael admired his newly purchased tools, gleaming in the sunlight. A beautiful shovel, a machete, organic herbicide, a six-pack of Gatorade, Francesco's finest boxed wine, and some kind of claw tool that looked like a medieval weapon. He was prepared to do battle.

A few hours later, Michael's bravado and excitement petered out. Kudzu was proving to be a worthy adversary. He gingerly removed his sweaty hands from his work gloves and leaned on the handle of his shovel. A constellation of puffy blisters dotted the bottom of his fingers. His shoulders ached, and his once proud, white, starchy socks now hung in soggy clumps around his ankles.

Michael took off his sweat-soaked hat. He'd finished off Francesco's best boxed wine and five bottles of Gatorade, and thoughts of giving up filled his head. He decided to seek inspiration by surveying his accomplishments. He counted eight lawn bags, each packed to the top with kudzu pieces and parts. He admired his de-vined fence and the fifteen-foot ditch that stretched across his yard. Every single inch of root had been removed.

"Rosemary, I'm doing this for you," he said, staring at the remaining ten feet of kudzu. Michael painfully pulled on his sweaty gloves, grabbed his shovel, and jabbed the titanium tip at the base of his willow tree, severing the vine. He crouched, straddled the vine, held the end, and heaved upward, ripping the roots from the topsoil. His hands rebelled angrily. He gritted his teeth, squatted again, and gave a tremendous tug. *Snap*!

Michael found himself sitting on the ground, legs sprawled, squinting out of his left eye. He lifted the bottom of his filthy, sweat-stained blue shirt, and wiped the dirt from his eye.

Between his legs lay a muddy ring…encircling a twisted piece of kudzu root. "My precious," he whispered. He studied the ring for a moment, and then, getting to his feet, grabbed his last bottle of Gatorade. He held the ring in his palm and poured the Gatorade over top of it, rubbing away the dirt with his fingers.

Michael's breath caught in his throat. It wasn't a root wedged into the ring…it was a finger, a human finger. Horrified, he took a step backwards, tripping over his shovel with a loud *oof,* sending the finger flying through the air.

"Oh no." Michael scrambled to his feet, scouring his yard for the finger. In the back of his mind, a thought clawed its way to his consciousness. *Where there's a finger…there's probably a body.*

Michael dropped to his hands and knees. He brushed his hands through the grass. Rosemary certainly hadn't prepared him for this in her gardening class. He grimaced when he finally located the finger. Picking it up like it was a deadly snake, he held it between his thumb and forefinger, arm outstretched as far as possible, and hurried toward the house.

Michael kneed the backdoor open, kicked off his boots, and ran through the utility room, slipping and sliding across the kitchen floor, his sweaty socks leaving a glistening trail behind him. He ripped a handful of paper towels from the roller and placed the finger in the middle of the stack.

Calm down. Gross! Calm down. Gross. Breathe…. Wash your hands and call the police. It's not like a few more minutes are going to matter to this guy.

Michael washed his hands, looked at the finger, and then washed them again. He grabbed a dish towel hanging on the front of the stove handle and wiped his hands dry.

Okay, I need to call the police and tell them I found a finger in my yard.

Michael snatched up his phone, Googled *Lana Cove Police*, and clicked on the telephone number link.

After two rings, an official-sounding person answered. "Lana Cove Police Department, may I help you?"

"Yes, yes…," Michael said breathlessly. "I just found a finger in my backyard…a human finger."

"Sir, did you say you found a human finger?"

"Yes," Michael answered. "A human finger, in my backyard."

"Who am I speaking with?"

"Michael West. I live at eleven-eight Ocean Crest Lane."

"Mr. West, are you at your residence?"

"Yes, in my kitchen."

"Okay, Mr. West, I'm dispatching officers immediately. Stay where you are."

"Thank you, Officer. Wait, sir, may I leave the kitchen?"

A belabored sigh filled Michael's ear. "Yes, I simply need you stay at your residence, until the officers arrive."

"Got it, thank you."

Michael hung up and stared at the finger lying on his counter. He'd watched enough *CSI Miami* to know that the most important thing was to preserve the evidence. Michael flung open a drawer, took out a Ziploc baggy, and gently dropped the finger inside. He sealed the top and placed the baggy in the freezer.

"Wait a minute, what if that destroys the evidence?" he whispered.

Michael picked up his phone and Googled: *Does freezing destroy evidence?* He combed through the results but found nothing specific to freezing and the destruction of evidence.

Michael exhaled. "The police are going to be here any minute." The words hung in space. He caught his reflection in the kitchen window. He looked filthy—filthy enough to bury a body?

That's ridiculous. No one would ever assume that I killed someone and buried them. If I had killed the person, why would I call the police? I would just leave them buried in my backyard.

Michael sprinted through the house to his bedroom, pulling off his clothes as he ran. He kicked his shirt and his shorts through the doorway of his bedroom beneath his bed and jumped into the shower.

The cold water washed over him. He exhaled and shivered. He didn't have time to wait for the water to heat up, the police would be arriving any minute. He filled his hand with shampoo, working it through his hair and then quickly using it on his face and body. He hastily towel-dried, threw on a fresh pair of shorts, a t-shirt, flip-flops, then finger-combed his hair. He'd just retrieved his dirty clothes from beneath his bed and thrown them in the hamper when there was a sharp *rap-rap* at his door.

Michael jumped. Even though he knew the police were on their way, the sharp *rapping* jarred his fragile nerves. It was the type of knock that meant business.

"Coming!" Michael shouted, jogging through the house. "I'm coming."

A phalanx of officers stood huddled together on his front porch, led by a broad-shouldered man in a navy-blue sports coat. His cheeks were pink and puffy as if someone had just tweaked them. A tiny crop of salt-and-pepper hair occupied the top of his head, like a bristle brush.

"Isn't it a little early for carolers?" Michael joked nervously. "Nothing? I'm sorry." He shook his head. "I tell jokes when I'm nervous—not that I'm nervous," Michael clarified.

"I'm Detective Adams." His voice sounded the same as a dry cough. "Are you Michael West?"

"Yes, yes, please come in," Michael offered, holding the door open.

"Thank you." Detective Adams stepped into the living room, deftly moving aside so the other officers could follow. He slowly turned in a small circle, taking in Michael's living room.

Michael followed the detective's eyes. From where he stood, he could see his dirty footprints, leading to his kitchen sink.

"So, Mr. West—"

"You can call me Michael."

"Mr. West," he repeated crisply, letting Michael know who was in charge. "You found a human finger?"

"Yes, I'm pretty sure it's a human finger. I was pulling up some kudzu in the backyard, and this finger flies out of the ground and smacks me in the eye." Michael pointed at his eye in case further clarification was needed.

"Talk about giving someone the finger," one of the younger officers said under his breath.

"I…I put the finger in the freezer," he continued.

"This just keeps getting better," another officer whispered.

"I really wasn't sure what proper protocol was," Michael continued. "I know if you lose a tooth you're supposed to put it in milk. When I was a kid, I knocked out my tooth, and my dentist said to put it in milk, and they were able to save the tooth, but honestly, I think the finger is too far gone."

Michael shifted uncomfortably when the young officer looked at the other and snorted.

Detective Adams sucked in his cheeks and released a lungful of stale air. "Mr. West, would you please show me the finger?"

Any other time, if someone had asked Michael to show him the finger, he would have gladly demonstrated the state bird of Massachusetts, but from the look on Detective Adams's face, it was obvious he was missing the humor gene. Michael would need to watch his mouth, or whoever it was in his backyard wouldn't be the only person missing a finger.

"Yes, sir, Detective. This way, please."

Detective Adams pulled a slender black pad from his pocket and scribbled a few notes as he followed Michael through the living room to the kitchen.

"This is a really nice house." Detective Adams smiled. "What is it that you do for a living, Mr. West?"

"I'm a writer," Michael replied proudly.

"Must be a pretty good writer to afford a house like this. Anything we may have heard of?"

"Well...." Michael paused. "I'm not really published yet. I'm still working on my first novel."

"I see, so unemployed," Detective Adams said and jotted 'unemployed' into his notebook. He glanced up from his notes and motioned for Michael to continue.

"You're wondering how I could afford this house," Michael stated.

Detective Adams met Michael's gaze but gave him nothing back.

"I've only been in Lana Cove for about three months now. Before that, I held a principal role at a prestigious advertising firm in Boston. I went through a miserable divorce, and I was looking for a fresh start. I used my savings to buy this house. I actually got a remarkable deal. It's the *only* way I could have afforded a house like this," Michael explained.

"Mhm...," Detective Adams said. "That's interesting."

Michael stared at him, dumbstruck. *Interesting is all he could conjure up?* "Here." Michael handed Detective Adams a cloudy baggy.

"You actually froze it," the detective said. He held the bag up to the ceiling light and then turned to the gaggle of officers. "Yep." He nodded. "That's a human finger. Wesley, get your men to work. All right," Detective Adams turned his attention back to Michael. "What do you say we start from the beginning?"

Michael stared out his kitchen window. CSI agents were busily setting up a command post, sealing off the area and erecting towering spotlights to illuminate the area where the finger had been found. A man in a white jumpsuit was kneeling, taking pictures.

"Mr. West," repeated Detective Adams, "why the sudden interest in digging up your yard?"

"Sorry, what?" Michael faced the detective.

The officer's lips stretched in a tight line. He tapped his pen agitatedly atop his notepad. "Try to pay attention, Mr. West. Why the sudden interest in digging up your yard?"

"Kudzu," Michael replied, "just like I told you earlier."

The detective stared at him, waiting.

"You're honestly asking me why I decided on *this* day to start digging up my yard? I didn't. I've slowly watched the vines smother my fence, my yard, and my willow tree, so I figured today was just as good as any day to take care of it." Michael bristled. "Do you go around asking people who happen to be gardening in their yard, why they decided to garden on that specific day, or perhaps plant a tree?"

"No," Detective Adams replied, "but then again, most people don't find a dead body."

"Finger," Michael corrected.

"In their backyard," Detective Adams continued.

The back door swung open with a bang, the doorknob slamming into the wall. A young freckle-faced officer cringed and mouthed "Sorry," and then focused on Detective Adams. "Sir, Margaret needs to speak with you."

"Thank you." Detective Adams spun on his heel, following the young officer out the door. He wheeled on Michael. "Don't go anywhere, we're not finished here."

"Wouldn't think of it," Michael said under his breath.

He stood at his back door. A woman in a white jumpsuit and blue gloves knelt on the ground where he'd been digging. An officer standing at the entrance to a taped-off barrier stepped aside as Detective Adams approached. Detective Adams nodded to the officer, fished a pair of latex gloves out of his pocket, and snapped them on.

The woman stood, bobbed her head, and then gestured toward a shallow rectangular hole. Michael guessed she was in her mid-forties, and her glasses had a light attached to the frame. Her hair was short, military short. She handed something small to Detective Adams.

Michael couldn't contain his curiosity any longer. He stepped out onto his porch. It appeared his neighbors couldn't contain their curiosity either. A crowd had gathered along the street, craning their necks and whispering.

Michael's next-door neighbor, Earl Cooper, and his wife, Tammy, rushed over to the white picket fence that separated their properties.

"Everything okay, Michael?" Earl called out.

Michael closed his eyes and exhaled. *What am I supposed to say? Everything's great, just a little homicide investigation.* Instead, he shook his head. "Not sure, Earl."

Detective Adams had ceased speaking with Margaret, the forensics officer, and was now watching him closely. Michael gave the detective a wan smile. He'd hoped the neighbors would give him some modicum of respect and let him have his privacy, but who was he kidding? His house was surrounded by a caravan of police cars, black SUVs, and a huge forensic van. Four massive spotlights shone brightly, illuminating his backyard. The entire site looked like a scene from *E.T.*

"Michael, what's going on?" Tammy squawked.

Michael sighed and walked over to them. "I was digging up kudzu." He motioned to the eight garbage bags.

"We saw," Earl confirmed.

"We were watching you through the kitchen window," Tammy added. "We weren't spying or anything, but how was that Francesco's boxed wine?"

"Not now, Tammy, this isn't the right time," Earl admonished.

"Sorry." Tammy nodded. "Maybe later…please, Michael, you were saying?"

"I found a human finger when I was digging up the kudzu."

"Oh." Tammy gasped and made a gruesome face. "That's horrible."

"Agreed," Michael said. "I called the police, gave them the finger. And then, this all happened." He indicated the activity behind him. "That's all I know right now."

"Creepy," Earl whispered, holding his phone up to his face, taking a selfie with the crime scene.

"What are you doing?" Michael asked. "Have some respect."

"It's cool, it's cool. I just posted a picture to the Lana Cove Community Watch page. There's a bunch of us who post to that website; it's how we keep our neighborhood safe."

"Obviously the system is flawed," Michael said flatly.

"You realize that there hasn't been a real crime—well, there's been petty theft and vandalism—but there hasn't been an actual crime here in Lana Cove since nineteen fifty-two when the Pritchett bank was robbed." Earl's voice quivered with excitement.

"I'm glad that I could bring a little excitement to the town."

"Was it a man's finger or a woman's finger?" Tammy touched Michael's shoulder. "I'm trying to ask delicately."

Michael looked at her, his face contorting. "I have no idea...I didn't see any nail polish."

A news truck screeched to a stop in front of his house. Michael's heart sank. He'd moved to Lana Cove to get away from the real world, to get away from the sirens and the harshness of the city, yet it seemed to have followed him here—to his own backyard.

"You should have sold tickets." Earl laughed and snapped a picture of the nosy neighbors. "You know, sometimes the murderer will show up in the crowds to see what's happening."

Detective Adams pointed at Michael and motioned him over. He met Michael at the edge of the barricade, a stretch of yellow tape dividing them.

"Mr. West, did you know a man named Herb Beaumont?"

"Yes," Michael stammered, his mind geared up, trying to make sense of the question he was just asked. "I mean, no. I mean, I didn't *know* him."

Detective Adams exhaled through his nose and narrowed his eyes. "Which one is it, Mr. West?"

"I bought this house from him. Well, not directly from him, because he was in France, but I bought it online. I worked with a local realtor, Maxwell King."

"Uh-huh." Detective Adams grunted, writing in his notepad again. "You said that Mr. Beaumont was in France?"

"Yes, he'd moved to France, and I was told he was buying a house there. He'd met someone and wanted to relocate there. He told me he needed to sell this house quickly, so I jumped on it."

Detective Adams stared at Michael for a considerable amount of time, not saying a word. Silence was powerful, and he knew if he waited long enough....

"You asked me how I could afford this house, well, that's how. You can ask Maxwell King—the king of real-estate guy."

"I know who Maxwell King is. So, you are saying that you never *physically* met Mr. Beaumont."

"Correct. I have *never* met him in person, I've never spoken to him over the phone. I emailed him a couple times when I had questions about the house, but that was it. Maxwell King arranged everything. You're welcome to check my phone records."

Michael wished he could see what Detective Adams scribbled in his notebook.

"Why all of these questions about Mr. Beaumont?"

"When was the last time you corresponded with Mr. Beaumont?" Detective Adams inquired, ignoring Michael's question.

Michael scratched his head. *When did I last correspond with him?* "About two months ago, I believe. I can check my emails. I emailed him to thank him for selling me this beautiful house, and I wished him well…in his new life in France. He didn't respond, and I haven't heard from him since."

"Interesting…. You see, Margaret, our chief forensic investigator, is saying, based on her preliminary analysis, that Mr. Beaumont was buried six months ago. So…," Detective Adams stared intensely at Michael, "I'm wondering how you were emailing a dead man."

"Gmail," Michael whispered.

"You think this is funny?" Detective Adams asked, his face growing tomato red.

Michael's mouth moved, but nothing was coming out.

"Cat got your tongue, Mr. West?"

"No, sir, I was simply saying I used Gmail—that's how we communicated. Maxwell King will confirm everything."

Detective Adams stared at Michael for what seemed like an eternity, and then walked away. He approached an officer, turned, and jerked his head toward Michael. Both officers looked at him and continued conversing. The officer pulled out his phone, and a few seconds later, he dialed a number. *He's calling Maxwell King to confirm my story.*

A cold chill washed over Michael. Was the body that they'd discovered really Herb's? It couldn't be. If that was Herb, then who had he been emailing?

Chapter 4

Questions and Answers

It was eleven o'clock before the circus left Michael's backyard. Detective Adams had grilled him for two straight hours. Michael was physically and mentally exhausted. He'd willingly handed over his laptop to the detective so he could access his emails to validate his story.

He tapped his worn notebook resting on his coffee table. He was glad he'd chosen to write his book manually rather than electronically—he had no idea when he was going to get his laptop back. Luckily, Michael's story had been completely corroborated by Maxwell King. Over the phone, Maxwell assured the police that Michael had never met Herb, and that he himself had only met him a couple times. Michael felt like he had been poked and prodded more than a pin cushion.

He plodded into the kitchen and stared at his white linoleum floor. His utility room, kitchen, and living room were caked in mud, soiled from the numerous police officers stomping through his house. He grabbed a bucket from beneath the kitchen sink, filled it with warm water, squeezed in some soap, and then got a mop from the utility room.

He had so many questions. *Who killed Herb and buried him in my backyard? How could they have done it?* He sloshed some water on the floor and methodically moved the mop back and forth. His hands instantly rebelled.

Earl and his wife are incredibly nosy. Surely they would have noticed someone burying a body in the backyard.

Who had he been emailing? His heart sank. And who had he bought the house from if that was Herb they found in his backyard?

Michael leaned the mop against the counter, opened the fridge, and picked up a Blue Moon beer. He'd clean the bucket out in the morning. He collapsed on the couch, held the remote, and turned on the television. He wasn't surprised to see the news was all about Herb's murder. Michael flicked off the television and closed his eyes and stuffed another pillow behind his head. Detective Adams's voice repeated in his mind: *Did you know Herb Beaumont? Have you ever met him?* He'd created a mental image of Herb, but in reality, he had no idea what he looked like.

Michael snatched his phone off the coffee table and opened Safari. He Googled *Herb Beaumont, Lana Cove, North Carolina*, and clicked the images tab. The results were disappointing, just a conglomeration of Lana Cove pictures that had nothing to do with Herb.

After an hour of searching Google and completely striking out, he gave up. He'd no sooner laid back down on his sofa when he sat up again. "Wait!" he exclaimed. "Earl!" Michael remembered Earl taking a selfie at the crime scene. Earl was Herb's neighbor. He took pictures of everything and posted them to Facebook. Just maybe….

Swiping his fingers across the screen, Michael tapped the Facebook icon and navigated to Earl's page. He clicked the photos tab. *Earl's quite the photographer. The last time Herb was seen was six months ago, when he originally left for France.* Michael backtracked through hundreds of images (mostly selfies of Earl) until he reached New Year's Eve, when a particular photo caught his eye.

In the picture, Earl and Tammy were sitting on either side of a white-haired gentleman. He appeared to be about sixty-five. Michael immediately recognized the painting of the bull and matador behind them. The photo was taken in the Cooper's living room.

The older gentleman's cheeks were bright red, and on the table in front of them were two empty wine bottles. A fourth person was taking the photo. Michael spotted the photographer's reflection in the golden frame of the painting; however, their face was hidden behind their phone. But the one thing that caught his attention was the caption beneath the picture: *Celebrating the New Year with our awesome neighbor, Herb.*

A shiver coursed through Michael's body—he'd found Herb.

Michael stared into Herb's eyes. It was so surreal, so incredibly strange to have been holding this man's finger.

He appeared truly happy in the photo, his eyes filled with light and merriment.

Why would anyone want to kill him?

Michael was just about to put his phone down when a picture of Earl and his wife, sailing across a cerulean blue sea, stopped him. "That's right." Michael nodded as if conversing with an invisible companion.

Earl and his wife had spent three weeks traveling through Italy, France, and Greece. He checked the date the picture was posted to Facebook, January sixteenth. *So, they probably left on the fifteenth....* *When did they return?* Michael quickly scrolled through the images until he reached one dated February fifth titled: *Au revoir, Paris.*

The timing fits.

The forensic expert said Herb was killed approximately six months ago. Earl and Tammy were Herb's only neighbor. If they were in Europe, it would have been the perfect time to kill and bury him without any witnesses. Michael yawned and closed his eyes. Sleep finally overtook his exhausted mind.

Michael jerked awake. His arm flailed numbly from beneath his pillow, knocking over his unfinished beer onto the coffee table. He quickly up-righted the bottle and rescued his notebook.

Morning sunlight filled the room, illuminating thousands of dust particles, floating like shimmering diamonds in the air. Michael rubbed his eyes and shook the cobwebs loose from his sleepy brain. He stared numbly at his phone as it vibrated itself off the coffee table onto the floor. Seconds later it chimed, alerting him that he had a voicemail.

Michael held the phone close to his face and squinted. He didn't recognize the number so he navigated to his voicemail. "Detective Adams," he moaned, looking at the transcript of the recording. He could already hear the man's Sahara-dry voice in his head.

Michael tapped the callback button, deciding he had better respond before Detective Adams decided to dispatch the entire Lana Cove Police Department on him.

Detective Adams answered on the second ring. He sounded tired. Michael wondered if he had worked through the night. He asked Michael to provide him with travel information over the last six months and then reinforced the fact that he wasn't to leave Lana Cove.

"Give me a call if you think of anything, no matter how insignificant it may seem."

"Yes, sir," Michael said, realizing Detective Adams had already hung up.

Michael padded barefoot to his bedroom, took a quick shower, and then hurriedly threw on a pair of khakis and a pale-yellow knit shirt. He wasn't feeling his usual tropical mojo.

There was no way Detective Adams believed Michael had any part in Herb's murder. It wasn't like he would kill Herb just so he could have his house.... *Please, if I was going to kill someone, I would at least make sure it was for an oceanfront mansion. I mean, if you're gonna kill someone, why not go all out?*

What Michael needed was some clarification. He needed to know where this left him. Had he been the victim of a huge con job? If the man he supposedly bought the house from was dead...then who had Maxwell King been corresponding with? Who had Michael been corresponding with? He grabbed his keys and stepped outside. First stop, Maxwell King, king of real estate.

Chapter 5

Maxwell King, King of Real Estate

Michael entered the garage through the side entrance and clicked the remote. The door shuttered and then groaned open at a soul-crushing speed.

Michael thought about banging his head on his steering wheel. Just as he began backing out, Earl appeared on his porch dressed in his maroon bathrobe and moccasin slippers.

Maybe he won't see me. Michael averted his eyes.

"Hey, morning, neighbor, beautiful day," Earl called out loudly, a huge grin on his face, as if he'd just caught a prized fish.

"Morning, Earl." Michael waved. He was convinced Earl had been stalking him. Most likely staring out his kitchen window, waiting for him to emerge.

"Get any sleep last night? Tammy and I were worried about you."

"Not a lot. You still read the newspaper?" Michael tried to redirect the conversation. "Very nostalgic."

"Some habits are hard to break…," Earl glanced at the folded newspaper in his hand.

"Well, enjoy." Michael smiled. "I've got to run some errands, busy morning." He shifted the car into reverse just as Tammy appeared on the front porch in a bright-pink fluffy bathrobe, a cup of coffee in her hand.

"Morning, Michael," she called out, waving.

"Morning, Tammy. I was just telling Herb—I'm so sorry, I mean Earl—I'm heading out to run some errands. Sorry again, just got Herb on the brain."

"Oh, bless your heart, I bet you do," she replied. "Such a mess." She shook her head.

Michael cut the engine and sighed. It was obvious he wasn't going anywhere fast. He climbed out of the car, walked over, and rested his arms on their shared fence.

"You guys knew Herb, right?"

"Of course." Earl nodded. "He lived beside us for…nearly seven years."

"Did he ever mention to you guys anything about moving to France?"

"No, I can't say that he did," Earl stated. "But Herb traveled a lot. Sometimes he'd be gone for weeks at a time, so we kind of got used to him coming and going. But," he shrugged, "the yard service was here every week, everything seemed normal, so we figured he was on an extended vacation."

"It wasn't until the moving trucks showed up," Tammy said, "that we realized he had moved."

"Didn't you find that odd?" Michael asked. "I mean, that he didn't mention he was moving?"

"It's just like we told that sweet Detective Adams. Herb was a very private person," Tammy said. "Don't get me wrong, he was friendly and all that, but he kept his personal life...well, personal."

"I guess...well...." Michael apologized, "Sorry for all the questions. Still trying to get over the fact that I buy a new house, only to find the owner buried in the yard."

"We understand," Tammy replied. "Never in our wildest dreams would we have imagined that something like this would happen. Herb was such a kind man."

"I feel a bit awkward even asking this, but you guys wouldn't happen to have a picture of him, would you? I've never even seen the man...," Michael lied.

Earl shot a quick look at his wife. Michael watched as she shifted the coffee cup to her other hand nervously.

"No, I'm afraid not." Earl smiled awkwardly. "Like Tammy said, we barely knew him, he was a very private man."

Out of the corner of his eye, Michael could see Tammy nodding in agreement with her husband.

"That makes sense," Michael said. "Okay...." He glanced at his watch. "I'm running late; have a great morning."

"You too, neighbor," Earl said.

Michael eased his car into the street. Something was up with his neighbors, but he couldn't quite put a finger on it. Earl had lied to him about taking a picture...but then again, he took a lot of pictures. Michael had scrolled through hundreds on Facebook. Maybe Earl simply didn't remember, or maybe he just didn't want to get involved. Maybe Michael was making something out of nothing.

He looked right then left, eased out onto Ocean Crest Lane, and then turned right on Sandpiper. He pushed his hand through his hair. His head pounded. It was eleven in the morning and he'd yet to have a single drop of coffee. He was pretty sure that was illegal in most states.

Michael wanted to talk to Ellie and Olivia. They had been there for him when he'd first moved to Lana Cove. They'd supported him through the emotional roller coaster of divorce and helped him fit into a new tight-knit community. But right now, what he needed was information, and the only person most likely to know the answers was Maxwell King.

Michael turned the corner onto Beachwood Avenue, passed the public library, and pulled onto a circular gravel drive. Real estate had obviously been good to Maxwell. His office was a gorgeous two-story coquina stone structure with beautiful framed windows across the front. Unless you knew better, you would mistake it for an elegant bed and breakfast. A simple gold plate on the door read: *Maxwell King, Realtor.*

Meetings with Maxwell were by appointment only, but Michael really wanted…needed a face-to-face—and honestly, he felt that Maxwell would blow him off if he called. Unfortunately, Michael knew he had nothing to offer the man but headaches. He pushed open the door and met with a whoosh of cool air, classical music, and the aroma of freshly brewed coffee.

Freshly brewed coffee air fresheners, is that a thing? If my book doesn't sell….

A tall, thin, blonde woman standing behind an equally tall desk glanced around her monitor at Michael. She smiled and held up a finger.

Just a moment, Michael interpreted her gesture in his mind.

Seconds later, the woman took off her headset and greeted Michael with a pleasant good morning.

"Good morning." Michael smiled. He liked her voice; it was rich yet effervescent. "I'm Michael West, one of Mr. King's clients," he clarified. "Is he in?"

"I'm sorry," she said, her face crestfallen, as if it were the worst news delivered in Lana Cove, ever. "He's at an appointment and—" She paused midsentence as the front door swung open.

An impeccably dressed man in a linen suit, the color of a golden pie crust, and a beautiful sky-blue necktie strode inside the lobby.

Michael recognized Maxwell immediately. He wore his salt-and-pepper hair short, like George Clooney, and he boasted a tan like George Hamilton—he looked like a man who spent entirely too much time on the golf course.

"Sir, this is Michael West. He said he is a client, but I don't see him—"

"A client?" Maxwell scoffed and shushed Kara's words away like a fly. "Michael, my boy." He rushed across the floor, grabbing him by both shoulders. "How are you holding up? Terrible news, this murder."

Michael wasn't sure what to do with his hands. Maxwell's were affixed to his shoulders. He wondered if he should raise them and pat Max's elbows, adding to the awkwardness.

"I just spoke with Detective Adams," Maxwell continued without letting him answer. "Look at those circles under your eyes. You need a day out on the golf course, get some sun in your veins." He smiled, revealing a mouth full of gleaming white dentures. "Kara, if you would, please, two cups of coffee. Cream, sugar, black?" he asked Michael.

"Cream and sugar would be perfect...." Michael directed his reply to Kara. "Thank you so much."

"Come, come." Maxwell motioned for Michael to follow him. He led him down a hallway filled with pictures of houses, awards, and floorplans, meant to impress prospective clients.

Michael paused in front of a picture of a massive oceanfront condo development. "Is that here? In Lana Cove?"

"You betcha. Beauty, isn't she? We'll start as soon as we get approval from the town council." Maxwell's face beamed with pride. "You're looking at Lana Cove's first high-rise."

"You're going to build a condo development?" Michael asked, baffled. "Here?"

"I know what you're thinking," he said, observing Michael's disapproving expression. "Trust me, it will be just what this town needs. All those elitist city folk will swarm to Lana Cove. It will be a virtual treasure trove of money. The locals may be crying now, but when the cash starts pouring in, it'll be a different story."

"I see," Michael said, still confused how such a monstrosity would be allowed in a community known for its quirky reclusiveness.

Maxwell threw his arm over Michael's shoulders. "Surely this isn't why you're here. I have an inkling you've got some questions for me."

Michael forced a smile and nodded, following him into his office.

"Take a load off." Max smiled and gestured to a spacious black leather couch that sat beneath a row of gold-framed awards. "So…." He parked himself behind a large wooden desk. "What's on your mind?"

"First, I'd like to apologize for bursting in on you unannounced like this, Maxwell."

"Nonsense, we're friends, Michael. You've got questions, and I've got answers. You weren't expecting a two-for-one deal when you bought the house, were you?" He laughed and rubbed his hands together. "Sorry." Maxwell must have seen Michael's pained expression. "That was insensitive."

"No, no, I'm sorry, that *was* funny…. I mean, under any other circumstance that would be funny."

"Thank you." Maxwell smiled again. Obviously, he was fond of his chicklet white dentures. "I like to think that I haven't lost my touch."

"I doubt that's possible," Michael offered reassuringly.

"Perfect. I have an appointment in about fifteen minutes. Let's get down to business."

"Yes, first I wanted to know if you have any advice as to where this leaves me."

"I'm not sure I understand…." Maxwell steepled his fingers beneath his chin.

"I'm trying to figure out if I actually own the house. According to Detective Adams, I most likely paid a con man…probably the man who killed Herb. So, I never actually paid the owner of the house, because the owner was dead."

"Let's not get ahead of ourselves, Michael. First of all, the police aren't sure that the person they found in your yard is Herb. Sure, they found a wallet, but that doesn't mean it's Herb. For all we know, the wallet could have been planted there."

Maxwell paused, and his eyes grew serious. "Michael, you know, that's how they grow money trees."

"What?" Michael asked, confused. "Oh, yeah." He nodded. "Money trees."

"Sorry." Max laughed and held up his hands. "I simply can't stop myself."

"It's okay." Michael smiled. "I have the same problem."

"Michael, my friend, there's a lot of investigating that needs to happen before any decisions are made. Months."

A light knock came at Maxwell's door.

"Come in, come in," Maxwell boomed.

Michael jumped up from the couch and helped Kara with the door.

"Thank you, Mr. West."

"Black onyx, with a precision-tooled gold rim. I had them handcrafted in Italy." Max declared, gesturing to the coffee cups.

Kara placed a coffee on his desk.

"Exquisite," Michael acknowledged. "They're gorgeous."

"The logo isn't painted on," Maxwell continued, "it's laser-etched with gold. I had a master calligrapher recreate my logo. It's truly a thing of beauty."

"A work of art." Michael turned the coffee cup in his hand, making sure he admired it enough to satisfy Max's ego.

Kara stepped out of the room for a brief moment and then reappeared with two miniature golden pitchers of crème and a brown bowl of sugar cubes. Michael was pretty sure—if Max could have—they would have been golden as well.

"Everything's organic and gluten free…. I'm not sure what gluten is, but we don't allow it in this office."

"I apologize." Michael glanced up at Kara. "But I'm organic intolerant. Do you have anything processed?"

Kara looked at Michael, bewildered for a moment, and then smiled. "Ah, very clever, Mr. West."

"Wonderful," Maxwell exclaimed. "Thank you so much, Kara. Please, if you would, hold my calls until we're finished in here."

"Certainly, Mr. King," Kara replied, closing his office door.

"My new agent." Maxwell filled his cheeks and blew out as if trying to whistle. "Trust me, once I get her trained up…."

Michael bit his tongue. Maxwell was showing his true disgusting colors. "She seems very nice and...." He struggled for the correct word. "Efficient."

"Right...," Maxwell laughed sarcastically. "You mean she's a knockout. Anyone with a pulse is going to be at her mercy. Men are gonna love her, and women are gonna want to be her. And she's all mine to mold and shape as I please."

Again, Michael smiled, amazed at how shallow this man was. Anger flashed through him as he thought about his daughter, away at college. He hoped he had prepared her for chauvinistic men like this. "Sounds like you've got it all figured out," Michael heard himself saying.

"You betcha."

"I know you've got a meeting in just a few minutes, but I highly respect your ability to read people, your intellect," Michael said to grease Max's ego. "You've been in this business a long time. Did anything seem out of the ordinary to you about this transaction?"

"Michael, I'm going to shoot it to you straight." Maxwell dropped a sugar cube into his coffee and swirled it around with a spoon. "Many times, older men, men like Herb, will do just about anything for love. The thought of your own mortality, growing old alone, without anyone in your life.... So when Herb called me—and let me add right now, if it wasn't Herb, it was someone who sounded exactly like him." Maxwell paused and took a sip of his coffee.

"He told me he'd met someone in France, the love of his life, his soul mate, whatever that means. I don't know about you, but I've had five or six soul mates. Anyways, he said he had found a little house in a seaside villa, and he asked if I could help sell his house."

Michael nodded, listening intently. "Have you ever done this before? I mean, sell a house when the owner's living elsewhere," he clarified.

"It's not something that happens frequently in a place like Lana Cove, but I've helped sell a few houses this way, mostly military folk."

"Okay, please continue," Michael prompted.

"Well, I told Herb I'd be happy to help him. It's a beautiful house, as you well know. And Herb graciously agreed to pay me my commission, plus a huge bonus if I could move it quickly. It seemed like a no-brainer."

"So," Michael said, deep in thought, "from what you are telling me, everything seemed legitimate?"

"Yep. He gave me power of attorney to draw up all of the documentation for the sale. I had complete control over the estate. I don't know, we probably talked on the phone a dozen times. I'm telling you,

like you said, everything seemed legitimate. Look,"
Maxwell said comfortingly, "he even emailed a
picture of him and the woman who he met, and the
villa in France. It was definitely him in the pictures.
I told Louie," Maxwell had clearly seen Michael's
confused look, "sorry, Detective Adams, that I had
no reason to believe it wasn't him."

"Yeah, everything sounds legitimate…. I guess
it will all depend on what the forensic team figures
out. Do you mind if I see the pictures he sent you? I
don't have a morbid fascination or anything, it's just
that I've never seen the guy," he lied.

"Sure." Maxwell motioned for Michael to join
him behind his desk. He tapped the spacebar on his
keyboard, waking his computer, and flipped over his
stapler. Taped to the bottom was a long string of
letters and numbers. "Kara changes it for me every
week. There's no way I could remember the crazy
thing."

Maxwell wiggled his mouse, found the pointer,
and double-clicked on a folder named: *Closed
Properties*.

"Here we go." He navigated to a folder named
Beaumont. He opened and expanded it, revealing
dozens of documents and photos of the exterior and
interior of the house.

Michael recognized the photos from the online listing he had seen when he'd originally bought the property.

"She is a beauty." Maxwell sighed, scrolling through the images. He finally stopped…. "Here." He opened one of the photos.

"That's Herb?" Michael stared at the white-haired man, a huge smile on his face, his arm around a beautiful woman with closely cropped, honeysuckle-colored hair.

Maxwell nodded. "That's definitely him."

"Well…he certainly looks happy." Michael leaned in, inspecting the image. Everything seemed legitimate.

Maxwell scrolled through two more images, both showing a stunning floral vista filled with small ornate houses. To Michael, it was like something you would find on a postcard.

"So, the money…. I mean, you were paid for everything?"

"Yes, the money was wired to an account at the *Société Générale*, a bank in France. I had a notice of receipt from the bank, and an email the next day that he'd got the money, and a few days later, the sale was completed. I received a wire transfer into my account for my fees…and my bonus. So, you can understand why I didn't suspect any wrongdoings…everything seemed…I hate to overuse the word, legitimate."

Michael stared at the last photo. He'd hoped that talking to Maxwell was going to help clear things up, but now his mind was filled with questions.

"You're just trying to figure out your next step." Maxwell patted Michael's arm. "You don't want to lose your house, and…you'd rather this all be far behind you. If I were you, I'd be doing the same thing."

"Yes," Michael agreed, "I don't want to lose my house, I'm just starting over."

"You're gonna be fine. As far as the law is concerned, they'll need to establish actual ownership of the property. I was the one who sold Herb this house seven years ago. That's why I imagine he approached me to sell it. Right now, *everything* points to you legally owning that house."

Michael exhaled a huge sigh of relief. "Thank you, Maxwell. That is extremely reassuring."

"Don't mention it. Listen, I golf with Judge Morris twice a week. I'll bend his ear a little bit and see what I can figure out for you. For now, let the police do their jobs. Lord knows they need the work." He smiled kindly and stood, letting Michael know the conversation was over.

Michael rose to his feet. "Thank you again, Maxwell. I truly appreciate your help."

"Not a worry, my boy." Maxwell placed his hand on Michael's shoulder. He walked with him out his office, down the hall, and through the lobby.

Kara was just finishing a phone call as they approached the front door. Michael turned and thanked her for the coffee. She gave him a *you're welcome* smile and then busied herself with a stack of folders on her desk.

"Thank you again for your help, Maxwell. I really feel a lot better."

"I'm glad I could help." Maxwell patted him on the back and held open the door for him. "Give me a holler if you need anything."

"I will," Michael called out and walked to his car.

"And, Michael…." Maxwell stepped onto the front porch, closing the door behind him. "I know I don't need to remind you, but let the police handle all this mess. And if I may, a friendly word of advice: Lana Cove is a unique place…. I wouldn't go snooping around if you know what I mean. People around here won't take kindly to it."

"I understand." Michael nodded. "Put it in the past."

"That's right; put it in the past," Maxwell agreed, nodding back.

Michael climbed into his car, put on his Ray-Bans, and slid his seat belt over his shoulder. He stole a glance toward the porch. Maxwell was still there, staring at him, an odd expression spread across his face.

Michael waved once again and slowly pulled around the horseshoe drive and eased onto Beachwood Avenue. In his rearview mirror, Max was still on the porch, watching him. Michael couldn't help but feel Max knew more than he was letting on.

Chapter 6

Don't Jump

Michael's brain was clouded with thoughts, like the sky above him. A storm was brewing. His phone buzzed, rattling the coins in his cup holder. He picked it up and glanced at the screen: *Olivia.*

She probably saw the news and is worried about me. He edged his way along North Street and turned onto Atlantic. By the time he arrived at the Bitter Sweet Café, the wind had picked up. A dark bank of storm clouds marched across the ocean. Lightning zigzagged in jagged arcs across the sky. Michael sat in his car for a moment, taking in the approaching tempest.

Ever since he was a child, he'd loved storms. Since moving to Lana Cove, he'd seen quite a few. Each one had taken him back to his childhood— staring out his front window; watching as the fat drops of rain splish-splashed onto his granite walkway; the bone-jarring boom of thunder that rattled the glass panes in his window, followed by the flash of lightning. He remembered his father telling him that there were ghost ships in the sky, and that the thunder and lightning were the cannons firing. A smile filled his face with him recalling his dad's words, remembering the magic, wishing it were true.

Michael pocketed his phone and climbed out of his Miata. A gust of wind blew across the parking lot, picking up sand granules that stung his arms and legs. A hat skittered by him, tumbling end over end. He glanced at the sky and estimated he still had about an hour before the storm made landfall. Plenty of time to grab a cup of coffee, a sandwich, and fill in Ellie and Olivia.

The café was busy with the usual lunch crowd. Michael paused in the doorway, trying to decide whether he should stay or come back later. Ellie was barely visible behind the crowd of people gathered at the counter.

He was about to leave when she glanced up from the mayhem and caught his eye. She winked at him, and that was all it took—Michael was staying.

He ignored all the stares. He could understand their curiosity—heck, he would've probably done the same thing. Here he was, a relative newcomer to Lana Cove, and he was already creating drama.

He'd lived through their initial hazing when he'd first arrived, and he was quite sure he could make it through finding a dead body in his yard.

Who knows, they may even be more respectful.

Any hope of respectfulness, maturity, or compassion flew out the window when the familiar raspy voice of Arthur Wisely called out his name.

"Hey, Michael…."

Michael sucked in his breath and turned to face the wrinkled octogenarian. He knew from the man's tone where this was heading. "Yes, Arthur?" he asked apprehensively.

"You know, if your book doesn't sell, you could always start an *herb* garden. Get it? An herb garden."

Michael rolled his eyes. "Really, Arthur, that's the best you can do? Did that one keep you up all night?"

"Nah, that was my bladder." He laughed and bowed his head, ingratiatingly accepting the smattering of appreciative applause that spread in a wave across the café. He took a victory lap around his table, high-fiving his friends.

"Please don't encourage him," Michael begged.

"Did you pour yourself a *stiff* one so you could sleep?" a little white-haired woman, sporting an

Italian race team biker shirt and pink riding tights asked. A huge grin engulfed her face.

"Mary Taylor!" Michael exclaimed, shocked. "You, too?"

"Well, they can't have all the fun," she replied indignantly and elbowed Arthur.

"Good afternoon. Michael."

"Thank God," Michael whispered, hearing Ellie's voice. It floated out to him like a well-tossed life preserver. He grabbed it and clung to it for dear life.

Her brown eyes brimmed with relief, seeing how Michael was handling the unruly crowd.

"I'm beginning to think that the people here don't like me," he said.

"They're just having fun. Besides, if they didn't like you, they would have keyed your car or knifed your tires by now."

"Should I be worried?" He stole a glance over his shoulder. "Arthur is looking pretty heated."

"Nah, don't worry about it, they took away his keys a long time ago."

"That's reassuring, because I'm pretty sure I saw him drive by my house yesterday."

"He has been known to steal, I mean, borrow other people's cars without asking on occasion, but he's harmless. Enough about him. How are you doing? I see you smiling, but are you really okay?"

"I'm good. Honestly," Michael insisted, aware of the crowd growing behind him. "I don't want to hold up the line. I'll grab some coffee and a sandwich and fill you in when you can catch a breather."

"Sounds good." Ellie smiled and eyed the line. "Good idea, the natives are growing restless." She affectionately touched the back of his hand. "Go find yourself a seat. I already know what you want."

Michael reached for his wallet.

Ellie stopped him. "This one's on the house."

Michael hesitated and then nodded. "Thank you, Ellie. I'm going to sit outside and watch the storm."

"You do that." She wrinkled her nose. "That storm is coming in quickly. Try not to get yourself killed—I don't need the bad publicity."

"Ah...," Michael laughed. "I'll do my best."

Michael leaned against the gray, sunbaked railing of the Bitter Sweet deck. It was deserted except for a small cluster of seniors playing cards.

He closed his eyes and relaxed. The air, perfumed with the smell of sea salt, tussled his hair playfully.

"Beautiful, isn't it?"

Michael recognized Olivia's voice.

"I love it when the ocean is that deep gray color."

"It's both beautiful," Michael agreed, "and foreboding."

"Ellie told me I'd find you out there. We both saw the news last night...horrible. I'm sure she asked, but are you doing okay? You seem okay," she added quickly.

"I'm doing a lot better than I was last night. I seem to have passed through the required stages of finding a dead body in your backyard pretty fast. At first, there was the shock phase, which was followed by the *how much wine did I drink?* phase. Then on to the *gross, I touched it* phase, then the *fear of being accused of a murder* phase, which I have to say can really spoil your evening."

"I bet," Olivia replied.

"Then the empowering acceptance phase that everything's going to be all right, and finally, where I find myself right now, the curiosity phase."

"That's a lot of phases. So, as I understand it, you are currently still in the curiosity phase."

"It's like trying to put a puzzle together without knowing what the completed picture is supposed to be—and with pieces from other puzzles mixed in."

"So, what have you figured out so far?"

"Well, for starters, I know I didn't kill Herb. I mean, that's something you'd most likely remember."

Olivia chuckled. "Yeah, I would imagine so."

"And if I didn't kill him, then I wonder, well, who did, and why? He had supposedly moved to France. Also, who was I communicating with if Herb was already dead?"

"Okay, you've confused me there. What do you mean by who were you communicating with?"

"You remember when I bought the house a few months ago?"

"Yes…and thank you for not saying 'it was rhetorical, I wasn't expecting an answer.' I hate it when they do that in the movies."

"Goes without saying," Michael agreed. "Anyways, Herb had moved to France, and I was emailing him back and forth about buying the house—except now, I know I wasn't emailing Herb, because he was dead. So, my questions are, who did I buy the house from, do I own the house, and who the heck was I emailing?"

"Oh yeah." Olivia nodded. "Good questions. Now I see why you are still in the curiosity phase."

"Yes, so I figured I needed to clear some things up. First, I wanted to make sure that I actually own the house—"

"Because you don't know who you actually paid," Olivia interrupted.

"Exactly," Michael replied, "and I wanted to find out if there was anything fishy about the sale of the house. So, I spoke to Maxwell King, you know, the king of realtors."

Olivia made a face at the mention of Maxwell's name but didn't say anything.

"According to Maxwell, everything was processed to the letter. His commission was paid, the house was paid for, he didn't see anything questionable. Max also said he'd corresponded with Herb by phone and email."

"Well, you know, you could always search to see where Herb's emails originated from, that would be a start…," Olivia offered nonchalantly.

"That's actually a great idea! How do I do that?"

"I have no idea, I've only seen them do it on those detective shows, but that being said, there's probably half a dozen YouTube videos that will teach you how."

"Brilliant." Michael cocked his jaw to the side and nodded.

"What are you two conspiring?" Ellie asked, placing a tray containing a coffee and a tuna melt on the table.

"Don't interrupt him," one of the card players yelled, "I believe he's about to jump." He pointed to the deck railing.

"And she's trying to convince him to do it," laughed another geezer.

"William Martin," Ellie berated. She leaned onto their table, narrowing her eyes at him. "Behave, or we'll begin discussing that little crush of yours on Mary Taylor. She's right inside." Ellie cocked her head toward the café lobby. "And she's feisty," she said, just loud enough for all of the men at the table to hear. "Understood?"

"Yes, ma'am," he whispered, his face turning bright red, to the delight of the other men who snickered like schoolchildren.

"The older they get, the pluckier they are." Ellie laughed and shook her head.

"Thank you for the coffee and…."

"Tuna melt," Ellie finished his sentence. "A complex blend of proteins and carbs. I figured you needed the protein." She paused. "The carbs, not so much."

"Uhm, thank you, that was really sweet of you, Ellie. You know, I'm happy to—"

"Oh my God, Michael." Ellie laughed again and rolled her eyes. "You're acting like I went out of my way and put the top up on your car or something."

"Yeah," Michael agreed. "Wait, what?"

"You left the top down, and these…," she held up a set of car keys, "lying on the counter."

"That's the first sign of old age, going out topless and forgetting your keys," Olivia remarked.

"It's when I start going out bottomless that we should all be worried," Michael said playfully.

"And on that note," Ellie exclaimed, "I'm back inside."

"Was it something I said?" Michael called out as she walked away.

"Just trying not to lose my lunch," she moaned and stepped back into the café.

"So," Olivia asked, "the police have pretty much cleared you?"

"Yeah. Do I detect a hint of disappointment? Did you want me to get arrested?"

"It's just that you're missing an amazing opportunity at getting a great set of headshots for your book sleeve."

"What are you talking about? I'm all about realism and research for my books but—"

"Matilda Watts is the police photographer, and she used to work for Glamour Shots, and I have to tell you, her mug shots are simply stunning."

"Wonderful, I'll keep that in mind next time I decide to go on a killing spree."

"Wear something blue," Olivia offered, "it'll make those eyes of yours pop."

"Blue, got it." Michael tapped his forehead. "You're a mess."

Olivia rested her head on Michael's shoulder. The card players had abandoned their post and moved their game inside. The first drops of rain were coming ashore.

"I'm glad you're okay, Michael. You're a complete nut, but Ellie and I think a lot of you. And...."

"There's an *and*?" Michael asked, smiling down at her—Olivia reminded him so much of his daughter.

"I'm just glad you didn't decide to jump."

Michael snorted at the unexpected comment and leaned over the railing, looking at the tumultuous drop to the ground some four feet below. "What? You're afraid I'm so old I'd break a hip?"

"Actually, I'm more concerned about you breaking your wrists. I'm counting on the royalties from your best seller to put me through grad school."

"That's a lot of pressure," Michael said.

"I know." She smiled, touching his shoulder. "But I'm worth it."

Chapter 7

I Get the Point

Michael sat at his desk listening to the rain beat against the windows of his cupola. He absentmindedly *tapped-tapped* his fingers on his desktop in chorus with the pitter-patter on the panes.

He moved his notepad aside, leaned back in his squeaky chair, and stretched his legs. He pushed himself away from his desk and slowly stood. He'd been distractedly writing for hours. He wasn't distracted from external elements, but from the internal clutter banging around in his head. He shook one foot then the other; they were numb from him sitting so long. *That can't be healthy.*

His notebook displayed a frazzled mind, the papers filled with eraser debris and cross-outs. A series of wet rings covered his desktop, from his watered-down glass of iced tea. A clump of lemon floated along the bottom like a dead fish.

Michael thought about the conversation he'd had with Olivia about tracking down where the emails originated. *Why does it even matter? It won't change anything.* Herb would still be dead. A con artist would still have his money, and it would only bolster the case against him, that he didn't own the house.

The sound of glass shattering startled Michael. He quickly looked around his office for a weapon. He pulled open his desk drawer and snatched up a miniature Louisville Slugger bat his father had given him as a child. He quietly descended the stairwell, his arm cocked back over his head, his bat at the ready. *I'll fake a head strike and then I'll smack him in the knees.*

He paused at the bottom, cringing as the step creaked and groaned under his weight. The backdoor flung open—whoever it was certainly took the term *breaking and entering* literally. Michael crept across the living room floor. *Wait, what am I doing? What if he has a gun?*

It was too late. The intruder dashed into the living room. Michael was caught off guard. A woman, her red hair chopped short—jagged bangs covered her forehead and one of her eyes—came to a stop directly in front of him. Michael recognized her expression, the look in her eyes: a cornered animal, an extremely dangerous cornered animal, with well-groomed eyebrows.

Michael lowered his bat. "Who are you, and what are you doing in my house?"

The woman seemed in no mood to answer. She took an aggressive step toward Michael.

He held out his bat and pointed it at her chest. "I think you need to leave before this gets ugly. I have a bat and I'm not afraid to use it." He waggled it at her, letting her know he meant business.

The woman stared, unblinking, at Michael, her hazel eyes, filled with something he couldn't describe. Suddenly, her fist cracked down, onto the base of his thumb. He dropped the bat and screamed—she shoved past him and raced down the hallway to the back of the house.

Michael chased after her into the guest room. She grabbed the closet door handle and yanked it open. Michael thought he might have a chance against her with her back turned to him. He gripped her by the back of her hoodie and jerked her away from the closet. She whirled on him and thrust a knife at his throat, jabbing it at his carotid.

Michael leaped back, smashing against the wall, holding his hands up. "What...what is this all about?" he stammered. "I think you've made a mistake."

"Shut up and don't move," the woman hissed, "or I will kill you." She knelt and ripped the carpeting up from the floor of the closet, revealing a wooden slat floor. She slammed the knife down, impaling the board. With a quick upward jerk, the board came free.

She deftly removed the knife from the board and stole a glance up at Michael, possibly making sure he understood that any funny business would end his life. She needn't have worried—Michael wasn't about to move. He had a major aversion to being stabbed to death and was quite sure she'd broken his thumb.

The woman leaned forward and reached inside the hidden compartment, extracting a small manila envelope.

Michael inched closer to see what she was doing.

She opened the flap and peered inside. From her expression and the expletive that shot from her mouth, Michael knew she hadn't found what she was searching for. He hoped she wasn't going to take her anger out on him.

She fished her phone out of her pocket, swiped to the flashlight app, and shone it down into the rectangular hole.

She cursed again and then, whirling on Michael, slapped him on the side of the neck with the dull edge of the knife. "Where's the key? Next time, I use the blade." She whipped the knife back, shoving Michael against the wall with her left hand.

"I-I don't know!" Michael stammered again. "I just moved here."

"There should be another piece of paper and a key," the woman snarled.

"I don't know!" The tip of the knife poked into his flesh.

"Has anyone else been here?"

"I have no idea. I mean, since when? I've had guests over, but…no one back here, not in this room, not that I know of. What key, what paper are you looking for?"

The woman glared at him; her eyes narrowed.

Sweat poured down Michael's face. "I bought this house from a guy named Herb…now he's dead…and I *really* don't know what any of this is about…." He gasped, catching his breath. "I really don't. Maybe Maxwell King, the realtor I bought the house from, has what you're after."

The woman took a step and pulled a photo out of the envelope and stuffed it into the pocket of her hoodie. She held the knife to his throat once again. "You feel the metal against your flesh, Mr. West?"

"Yes, yes."

"One word of this to anyone, and I will kill you in your sleep." She withdrew a lighter out of her pocket and put the flame to the corner of the envelope. The old paper immediately caught fire. She held it until the flames licked at her fingers and then tossed it into a wire trash bin.

"Not a word," she growled, and without a glance back, she raced through his house and out the back door, into the night.

Michael rushed over to the trashcan and flipped it over, extinguishing the fire. Luckily, the trashcan had been empty. If it had been his office one, filled with scraps of writing throwaways, the entire house would have gone up in flames.

Michael stared down at his hands; they were trembling. His thumb was twice the size of his other one. *If I ever have to hitch a ride, I won't have any problems.*

He leaned over and picked up the remaining scrap of smoking envelope. Not much had escaped the fire—a fragment of an address, and on the upper corner of the envelope, a curled stamp clinging for dear life. Michael walked through the living room and lay the charred remains on his coffee table. He'd inspect them more closely, but right now, he had to repair the broken window in his back door.

Thirty minutes later, Michael stepped back and inspected his handiwork. A triangular piece of cardboard affixed to the doorframe with duct tape. He grabbed his broom and finished sweeping up the broken shards of glass that lay scattered across the utility room floor.

He snatched his phone off the kitchen counter and was about to text Ellie and Olivia when the woman's voice spoke in his head. *She said if I tell anyone, she'll kill me.* He exhaled. *I don't want to do anything that could endanger their lives.* He took a freezer bag out of the drawer, filled it with ice, and then placed it on his thumb. *Well, that's ironic.* It was the second time he'd put an appendage on ice.

He padded barefoot into the living room, sat on the couch, and slid his notebook onto his knees. He wrote *timeline* at the top of the page and then recreated the events leading up to the present.

I purchased Herb's house at the end of February and moved in, in March. I found Herb's body in the backyard in June.

Michael tapped his pencil on his forehead. "At least we think it's Herb's body."

But then again, everyone's basing his identity on his wallet.

Michael made a note to check with Detective Adams if they'd decided if it was Herb or not.

Maybe it wasn't. Maybe Herb was alive and well in France living out his dream…highly unlikely, but strange things did happen. Michael repositioned the ice pack on his thumb.

Wait…didn't Max have pictures of Herb alive and happy with his new love interest, in the French villa? But…those pictures could've been taken at any time, plus, who knows who the woman is really—she could have been Herb's daughter for all we know.

"Okay." He sighed. "Back to my list."

Strange red-haired, hazel-eyed woman breaks into my house and threatens to kill me if I don't give her a key. She's obviously been in the house before, because she knew exactly where to go.

Underneath his quick timeline, he wrote the word *questions* and underlined it three times for emphasis.

Was the red-haired woman a friend of Herb? If so, what was Herb hiding? Is that what got him killed? Why was the woman so panicked? Did she just find out about Herb's death from the news?

He put his pad down on the coffee table and picked up the scorched envelope. A startling *bang, bang, bang* at his front door had him jumping to his feet. *Is she back?* He hid the envelope remains under his couch cushion.

A fist pounded heavily at his front door. "Michael West!"

Michael recognized Detective Adams's voice.

"Open up; it's the police."

He shuffled to the front door and threw it open. "Detective Adams, what's going on?"

Detective Adams pushed past Michael and strode into his living room, his eyes probing every inch. "What's that burning smell?"

"Incense," Michael said. "Very cheap incense."

Detective Adams whirled on Michael. "I'm not here to play games with you. Where have you been all evening?" His voice was arctic.

"What is this all about? You barge into my living room and start asking questions." Michael threw his hands up in dismay. "Here. I've been here, writing." He gestured to the notepad on the living room table. "Doing research for my new book, *Killer Canvas*."

Michael wished he'd hid his notebook as Detective Adams's gaze settled on it.

"Why are you asking me all these questions?" Michael asked in an effort to draw the detective's attention away from the notepad.

"Do you own a red Miata, Mr. West?"

"Spector?" Michael's shoulders slumped. He didn't like where this line of questioning was going. "Yes," he offered hesitantly. "Why?"

"Mr. West," Detective Adams plowed on, ignoring Michael's questions, "where is your vehicle?"

"In my garage. I have to keep it in the garage because of the oak tree by the driveway. The birds like to use it as a launch pad to dive-bomb my car."

A crisp "Show me," was all Detective Adams replied.

"Sure." Michael slipped his bare feet into a pair of black flip-flops and walked to the door. He hesitated for a moment—the hook where he kept his keys was empty.

"Is there a problem, Mr. West?" Detective Adams asked, noticing Michael's hesitation and the empty hook. "Mr. West?" he asked again.

"No…," Michael paused. He turned and smiled at the detective. "One second, let me get my garage remote." He hurried through the kitchen, checked the table and the kitchen counter. *I know a put the keys on the hook.* He quickly replayed the events of the past few hours. *I left the café, came home, parked the car, grabbed my mail, came in the front door, hung my keys…. Yes, I remember, I hung them by the door.* He slipped into the utility room and picked up the garage remote.

"Got it," he called out and headed back into the living room.

Detective Adams held open the door for him, gesturing for Michael to continue ahead of him. Two more officers stood in his driveway. His neighbor's lights flicked on. Their kitchen window was reflected in a puddle on the drive. He glanced up just as Earl and Tammy ducked, in an attempt to not be seen.

"Great," Michael muttered.

A fine mist filled the air, his shirt clinging to his body.

He clicked the remote and waited along with the officers while the garage door slowly rose. A sigh of relief escaped his lips when the wheels of his car appeared. It hadn't been stolen. His joy, however, soon turned to dismay when the door had fully risen. The front end of the Miata was crushed. Remnants of blue paint were on the bumper and along the passenger side of the car. Long deep grooves that could only happen when metal met metal extended the length of the car.

Michael looked at Detective Adams, dumbfounded. "What happened to Spector? What is going on?" Michael started for his car, but a police officer grabbed him by his shoulder.

"That's far enough, sir."

Michael shook his shoulder free and faced Detective Adams. "What happened to my car? It was fine when I put it in the garage this afternoon."

"I'm sure it was," Detective Adams replied. He swiped across his phone and then turned it toward Michael so he could see the screen. "Do you recognize this woman?"

Michael swallowed hard. It took a moment for his eyes to focus. His head snapped back in shock— it was the woman. The woman who had threatened him with the knife, only now she had a large gash on her forehead, her hair was a wet, tangled mess, and her hazel eyes stared into a void, no longer a part of this world. She was dead.

Michael felt dizzy. He stood unsteadily, swaying. "No," he whispered, "I don't know her. Is she…?"

"Dead, yes, she's dead. Her car was forced off the road into the Halifax River…an anonymous witness described your car and your license plate."

"It might have been," he glanced uneasily at his car, "my car that was involved in the crash, but it definitely wasn't me driving it."

"What happened to your thumb?" Detective Adams asked, jutting his jaw at Michael's left hand.

"Oh that, it's not really my thumb…. I mean, of course it's my thumb. I meant it's my wrist and thumb, together. I have really bad carpal tunnel. I usually wear my brace when I'm doing a lot of writing."

"Mhm." It was clear Detective Adams didn't believe him. "People keep turning up dead around you, Mr. West."

"Look, someone stole my car. It's obvious they're trying to frame me for Herb's death, and now this *poor* woman." He struggled with the word poor. Just a couple hours ago she was jabbing a knife at his throat.

"Mr. West, I'm going to need you to come into the station for questioning. CSI will need to do a forensic sweep of your car. Officer Morris and Chester will give you a ride to headquarters."

"I'm not sure I'll be any help. May I put on some shoes?"

"Michael," Detective Adams said, "I don't think you did this, but you seem to be inexorably entangled in whatever's going on."

"I appreciate that, sir, I'll do whatever I can to help." It didn't escape Michael's attention that was the first time Detective Adams had called him by his first name.

"You can start by telling the truth."

Michael didn't have to see Detective Adams's face. He already knew the detective realized he wasn't being forthcoming about everything.

"About that," Michael said. "I noticed when I walked by the door that—"

"Your keys were missing," Detective Adams interrupted. "I know, I saw you hesitate at the door, and the empty key hook. Either the thief kept them, or if we're lucky, we'll find them somewhere in your car."

"Fair enough." Michael nodded. "I'll grab my shoes."

Chapter 8

Texting Texting 1-2-3

Michael eased his rental, white BMW M4 convertible onto Main Street. It had been a long night, one that he hadn't planned on spending at the police station drinking lukewarm coffee from a Styrofoam cup. He hoped he'd made the right decision by coming clean with Detective Adams about the mysterious woman. He'd come to the conclusion that it would be better to make a friend than a powerful enemy.

As the night wore on, Detective Adams's demeanor had softened. Michael apologized for withholding information about the woman—he reiterated his reasoning: she did threaten to kill him if he said anything about her. However, now that seemed a moot point.

The writer in him appreciated the fact that Detective Adams took a lot of notes. He scrawled quickly, some kind of illegible secret code that probably only made sense to him. Michael concluded from his penmanship, Detective Adams was either born to be a detective or a doctor. Most likely a proctologist.

He asked Michael to give him one more final run-through of the past twelve hours. He stopped Michael, asking for more details about the secret hiding place in the closet and the envelope with the picture. Michael did leave out the part about keeping the charred remains under his sofa cushion. The detective asked once more about the missing key, to which Michael posed a question to him: "Were any keys found on Herb's body?"

Detective Adams said they hadn't found any keys, just a candy wrapper and his wallet.

After finishing up with Detective Adams, officers Morris and Chester had given him a ride home. They'd even walked through his house with him, checking in closets, the shower, cabinets, and his garage, making sure there were no uninvited guests.

Surprisingly, Michael had slept through the night. He was sure he was too amped up to sleep, but as soon as he closed his eyes, he fell into a deep slumber. He'd awoken that morning to a vibrating buttock—it was Ellie calling to make sure he was okay. That was where he was heading now, to the

Bitter Sweet Café. He needed coffee, lots of coffee, and a makeup artist from Sephora.

Michael glanced up bleary-eyed at the rearview mirror. He looked awful. Dark circles beneath his eyes, his hair seemed like he'd gotten in a fight with a weed whacker, and his five o'clock shadow had turned into a jaw-shaped shag carpet—at least he'd remembered to brush his teeth. He let out a loud yawn, to the pleasure of the children in the car beside him. They pointed and made faces at him as they drove off.

I deserved that.

Michael turned onto Atlantic Avenue. It was a beautiful morning. Cyclists were speeding along the sidewalk dressed in their finest Lycra shorts and sponsored t-shirts. A group of seniors streamed by, colorfully clothed and properly hatted to protect their heads from the sun, proud members of the Lana Cove speed-walkers group.

Don't laugh, that will be you someday, with your white compression socks stretched up to your knees.

He drove into the Bitter Sweet Café parking area just as Arthur Wisely rode in on his pastel-blue recumbent bike, complete with a massive mirror that could compete with the Hubble telescope.

"Nice car, Michael," he said admiringly, caressing it with his eyes.

"Don't get any ideas," Michael warned, "I've heard about you."

Arthur wiggled his eyebrows and gave Michael a devious smile. "Who, little old me? I'd never, not when I've got this beauty." He stroked his gleaming chrome handlebar.

"You're a strange man, Arthur."

"What happened to your flame-red midlife crisis on wheels?"

"I'm having it professionally detailed, you know." Michael grinned. "To get rid of that pesky evidence."

Arthur's jaw dropped. Michael was quite sure it was the first time, since he'd known him, that he'd seen Arthur speechless.

"Have a nice day," Michael called out as he stepped into the Bitter Sweet Café.

He paused in the doorway, straightened his shirt, and ran his fingers through his hair. Michael Buble's sweet tenor voice blended with the smell of fresh cinnamon buns. The aroma was so decadent, Michael felt himself gaining weight by just inhaling.

A largish woman, her red hair in a tangled bun, leaned onto the counter, as if it were an old country fence. She was conversing loudly with Ellie. Ellie's face lit up when she saw Michael standing in the doorway.

The huge woman peeled her forearms from the counter, making a sound like sweaty skin on a leather couch, and turned to see who had caused the sudden change in Ellie's demeanor.

"If it isn't Michael West, marketing maven, color neophyte." The woman's huge eyes opened even wider. "I'm disappointed. No Magnum-wear today? I betcha only save that shirt for special occasions?" She snorted at her own joke.

"Gail, so wonderful to see you. Sorry, no sexy shirt for you today. Ellie told me that the sight of my chest kept you awake for days."

"Michael," Ellie gasped, "I did not—"

"So," Michael continued unabashedly, "I thought I'd dress a little more conservatively on your behalf."

"He is a riot." Gail laughed. She patted Michael on the chest. "I'm sorry, darling, but you don't have enough stamina to keep me up at night."

"What? What's that supposed to mean?" Michael asked, insulted.

"I'm going to give you lovebirds some alone time. Ta-ta," Gail chirped and waved her hand over her shoulder.

"You have the strangest friends." Michael turned back to Ellie. "Present company excluded, of course."

"Life is like a box of chocolates," Ellie said sagely.

"You never know what you're gonna get," Michael smiled, finishing her sentence.

"Oh, the glorious wisdom of Tom Hanks." Ellie sighed. A timer chimed behind her. "Wait one second." She swiveled and took two freshly baked cinnamon buns off the rack with a pair of tongs and placed them into a white cardboard box. She reached above her head and grabbed two mugs and filled them with coffee.

"Let's talk outside," she offered as she stirred skim milk into Michael's cup. She slid the coffees across the counter to him and then scooped up the box with the cinnamon buns and collected some napkins.

"Jeff," she called out to a thin millennial in black skinny jeans, "watch the front, I'm stepping out for a few."

"You got it, Miss Banks."

When they'd taken a seat outside, Ellie's demeanor became more serious. "I struggled with whether I should show you this or not." She tapped her finger on the table.

"Ellie," Michael said, his face filling with concern, "what is it?"

She reached into her pocket and slid a folded piece of paper across the table to Michael. He carefully opened it and read the handwritten message.

Think twice about who your friends are. It could be bad for business. Very bad.

Michael sighed. "I'm sorry, Ellie. Do you have any idea who wrote it?" He continued before she could answer. "Maybe I should just stay away, you know, until things blow over. I am a suspect in two murder cases."

"Don't be ridiculous, Michael," Ellie exclaimed, making a face, "it's just somebody trying to stir up trouble."

"You can't really blame them, Ellie. They're just trying to protect you. Some simply need a little more guidance." Michael slid the note back to her.

"It doesn't help that your neighbor, Earl, posted pictures of the police at your house last night, and CSI towing your car away—on the Facebook neighborhood watch page."

"You're kidding me!" Michael exclaimed angrily. "That guy's a menace."

"A little birdy told me that, ever since you found Herb in your backyard, Earl has been seen playing golf and dining out with Maxwell King. It seems that Earl wants to make a play for your house."

"By turning the townsfolk of Lana Cove against me? It's gonna be like the Salem Witch Trials."

"Except you're too pretty to be a witch," Ellie said gently.

"Well, that's true," Michael agreed. "The truth is, Maxwell said everything was done legally. All financial obligations were met. And," he added, remembering his conversation with Detective Adams, "the forensic people are still waiting for the DNA analysis. Herb may be alive and well, living in France for all we know; we simply have no idea where."

"I'm just trying to give you a heads-up," Ellie explained. "Earl and Tammy are not looking out for your best interests. If they can turn the town against you for their benefit, they will."

"I appreciate that."

A gust of wind blew across the deck, sending a clutch of flyaways across Ellie's face. She brushed the hair from her eyes.

A sudden sadness filled his heart. "Ellie, maybe I should keep my distance. You and Olivia have a business to run, you don't need the distraction of—"

"Michael," Ellie said hotly, "I'm sorry, but I do not turn my back on my friends, especially when they are being treated unjustly."

"Okay." Michael held up his hands. "But please listen to me."

Ellie's phone vibrated. She tilted her phone so she could see the screen. "One sec, Michael, it's Liv."

Michael waited impatiently for her to finish the call. He needed Ellie to understand the seriousness of the situation. He was touched that she supported him, but he was quite sure none of her other friends had been a suspect in two murder investigations.

"Olivia's five minutes away," Ellie explained. "If you don't mind, I'm gonna put the phone on speaker so she can listen in."

"Morning, Olivia," Michael said with as much enthusiasm as he could muster.

"Morning, Michael." Olivia's voice was always effervescent. "You two keep talking, just pretend like I'm not there, contemplating your *every* spoken word."

"Okay." Michael sighed. "Whoever is involved in all of this mayhem is dangerous. The woman they found last night in the Halifax River...someone stole my car and rammed her off the bridge."

Ellie nodded. "I know, I kind of put two and two together."

"Me too," Olivia added, "though I never would have thought of using a Miata to ram another car off the road."

"Anyways, that same lady broke into my house last night and threatened me at knifepoint."

"What?!" Ellie exploded; it was her turn to be surprised. "You could have been killed! What did she want?"

"It's okay," Michael reassured her. "I had my baseball bat, if things got too ugly."

"You?" Ellie shook her head. "You of all people were going to hit her with a baseball bat?"

"It was a miniature bat, you know, the novelty kind?"

"Oh, Michael, is that what happened to your thumb?"

"What's the matter with his thumb?" Olivia asked.

"It's only black and blue and puffy," Ellie declared.

"I have carpal tunnel—"

"Did she break your thumb?" Olivia asked. "How are you going to write?"

"She punched me in the thumb, okay, you happy? I wasn't expecting her to punch me in the thumb. She used some kind of ninja strike to knock the bat out of my hand."

"I'm here," Olivia said. The *tick-tick-tick* of her blinker came over the line. "Don't say anything else until I get there!"

"Do you want some ice?"

"No, just my dignity," Michael said, crestfallen.

"Michael, I think you know it's much too late for that."

Olivia held the door open for a family, a mom and dad and three children. They commandeered a table by the railing. The children immediately climbed onto the chairs, standing so they could watch the ocean as they ate.

"Hi, guys." Olivia waved, rushing to the table. She leaned over and gave Michael a shoulder hug and kissed Ellie on the cheek. She pulled a blue scrunchie from her wrist and wrapped her hair into a loose ponytail.

"Okay." Olivia tore a huge chunk off of Michael's cinnamon bun. "Keep going."

"Where was I?" Michael inquired.

"The lady had just punched your thumb." Olivia grimaced at the sight of Michael's swollen appendage.

"Right, so the woman had obviously...." Michael paused while Olivia grabbed his coffee and took a huge swig. "You gonna be okay?" he asked.

"Sorry, I'm famished, too many errands this morning."

"Here." Michael slid his cinnamon bun over to Olivia. "I've had about fifteen cups of police coffee and two packs of stale, orange, peanut butter crackers from a vending machine."

"I'll just run in and get another bun, I can't take yours," Olivia insisted while shoving another huge chunk in her mouth.

"All right." Michael still pushed his coffee and plate over to her. "So, the woman had either been in my house before, or she'd researched the layout. As soon as she came in, she made a beeline for the spare bedroom."

"First time that's ever happened." Olivia snorted. "Sorry," she muttered.

Ellie reached over and patted her hand. "It's okay, Liv, I was thinking the same thing."

"May I finish my story?" Michael looked from Ellie to Olivia, who both nodded. "Thank you. So, I chased after her; she opens my closet and yanks up a board that's hiding a secret compartment."

"Oh." Olivia gasped. "What was inside?"

"If you say Jimmy Hoffa," Ellie warned, "I'm gonna be pissed."

"Look, a woman has been murdered, and you think I would stoop that low?"

"Well, when you put it that way," Ellie said sheepishly.

"It was Elvis," he deadpanned.

"I knew you couldn't do it." Ellie moaned. "All right, so what did she find?"

"An envelope with a picture in it."

"Did you see the picture?" Ellie asked.

"No, she stuffed it in her jacket, but she went ballistic on me because there was supposed to be a key in the envelope, too, and it was missing."

"A key," Olivia said as if it were the most mysterious thing in the world.

"And let me guess, she thought you took the key?" Ellie asked.

"I don't think so. I told her I didn't know anything about a key. I said maybe Maxwell King might know if a key had been left behind, because I had just bought the house from him."

"And she believed you?"

"Yeah, I'm pretty sure…. She put her knife to my throat and said if I told anyone about her, that she would kill me in my sleep, and then, poof, she was gone."

"Well," Olivia declared, "that's probably the best way to go, being stabbed in your sleep."

Ellie clutched her coffee between her hands and leaned back in her chair. Michael wished he'd clutched his cinnamon bun that way. The only surviving piece was a glistening golden crumb on Olivia's lips. Which she licked away seconds later.

Michael wasn't sure if it was his stomach growling or if he had a message. He glanced at the screen. It was a text from Kara, Maxwell King's assistant. Michael stared at the text, baffled.

"What is it?" Ellie asked, seeing his confused expression.

"If you make the font bigger, you can read it more easily," Olivia suggested.

"It's Kara; she's Maxwell King's assistant," Michael explained. "She says that she has some tax paperwork that I need to sign, and she's insisting that she meets me at my house."

"Well, that seems odd." Ellie took a sip of her coffee. "Why at your house, not at the office?"

"I agree with Ellie," Olivia chimed in.

"I'll tell her I'm near her office and I'll just swing by." Michael shrugged.

"Here," Olivia said, grabbing his phone, "you see this little guy?" She pointed to the microphone icon at the bottom of his text. "Tap that and speak instead of hunting and pecking."

Michael tapped the microphone. "Oh cool.... Look!" He held out his phone. It had typed, *Oh cool.*

Olivia rolled her eyes and crossed her arms. "Welcome to the twenty-first century."

"Sent," Michael announced proudly. A few seconds later, his phone vibrated. "We need to talk," he read, "in private, without Max."

"Michael, you can't meet that woman there alone. If she turns up dead, it's not going to look good. I'm going with you," Olivia said.

"If she has information, and she knows you're there, you may spook her away. I'm not sure it's a good idea," he said.

"She won't even know I'm there," Olivia insisted.

"Are you sure? I think I'll be fine."

"Me thinks thou thumb dost protest too much." Ellie nodded at Michael's hand.

"Fine." He sighed. "Since you've moved from quoting Hanks to Shakespeare, I guess I have no other option."

"Wonderful, text her and tell her to meet you in half an hour. That way you can get home before she does," Ellie suggested.

"All right." Michael fired off the text to Kara.

Ellie sprang from the table and dashed inside ahead of them. By time they made it to the counter, she was holding another cardboard box. "Here's a couple for the road," she said, handing the box to Michael. "You look like you need it."

Chapter 9

The Silver Key

Michael stood at the living room window sipping a cup of coffee. He tapped his foot nervously. Kara was risking a lot by coming here, especially with his nosey neighbors. *Maybe that's what she wants to talk about.* His heartbeat quickened. *Maybe she's going to tell me that Earl and Max are working out some secret deal to take my house.*

A midnight-blue Lexus pulled along the curb and came to a stop just beyond his mailbox. Michael ran back to his guest bedroom. Olivia was kneeling on the floor, peeking through the blinds.

"She's here," Michael said quietly.

"I see. Be careful, Michael."

Michael resumed his position at the window. A tall elegant woman with black hair, white oval sunglasses, and a sleeveless black-and-white sundress stepped out of the car and sauntered up his driveway, like she was walking the red carpet.

Michael hurried over to the door and held it open for her. "Good morning," he exclaimed as she went inside.

She turned slowly in his living room. The sunlight shone through the window, her skin glistening. "I'm sorry that I had to be so secretive about our meeting, Mr. West."

"Please, call me Michael. The wig, I must admit, is a nice touch."

"You think so? I thought it was a bit garish, but you have nosey neighbors, Michael—as you already know."

"Is that what this is about? Earl and Tammy?"

"No, but you are right to be concerned. Given the opportunity…." She let her voice linger. "My visit is about this." She held a silver key in her palm.

Michael jumped back as if she were holding a snake.

She looked curiously at him. "It's just a key."

"That key and I have a long history, which I can't get into right now."

Kara raised a groomed eyebrow. "Michael, when Herb left for France, Maxwell was searching for something. He removed light switches, electrical outlets; he removed the bathroom and kitchen pipes, you name it. My guess is he was looking for this."

Michael nodded. "He was obviously searching for something. So, how did you wind up with the key?"

"I found it hidden within a light fixture."

"And you decided not to give it to Maxwell? Why?"

"Believe me, I've wrestled with whether or not to give it to him. But in the end, I listened to my inner voice. It told me to wait, to bide my time."

"And so your inner voice is telling you to give *me* the key?"

"Michael, I think you and I both know that Maxwell King is not a good man. I would go as far to say that he is evil." She reached out and took Michael's palm and dropped the key in his hand. "I believe that you are a good man, Michael, and that you will find the answer behind this key."

"I don't even know where to start. Are you sure this is a good idea?"

Kara's phone vibrated. Her face paled when she glanced at the screen. "Excuse me for one moment." She swiped her finger down her phone and pressed. A look of panic filled her eyes. She tapped her phone again. "Michael, I'm dreadfully sorry to ask, but may I use your cell? I can't seem to get a signal, and this is a bit of an emergency."

"Certainly." Michael grabbed his phone, tapped in his code, and handed it to her.

"I'm just going to step out on the porch a second. It's a little sensitive. I hope you understand?"

"Yes, please, take your time."

"Thank you." She opened the door and stepped outside.

The urgency in her voice was evident as she talked.

A minute or so later, she stepped back into the house. "Thank you, Michael." She handed him back his phone. Her hands were trembling.

"Kara, is everything okay?"

"I'm so sorry, I apologize."

Michael stood aside, and Kara bolted out. He stood in the doorway. She didn't bother to put her seat belt on as she sped away.

Olivia joined him in the living room. "That was Kara? She's gorgeous."

"Yes," Michael answered without looking up. He was staring at the silver key in his hand.

Chapter 10

Bramston Young University

Olivia turned the silver key over in her hand. "That's the strangest key I've ever seen." She traced her finger over a little green plastic circle located on the bow of it. "It says ABLOY."

"Kara risked a lot coming here. I mean, Earl could have seen her, and we both know his first call would be to Maxwell."

"Didn't you say she was in disguise? Maybe Earl will think you just had someone *special* over."

"Great." Michael threw up his hands. "I'm sure he'll post that to the community crime watch page, too. At least...," he glanced at the ceiling and squinted, "I don't recall seeing a midnight-blue Lexus at Maxwell's office. Hopefully, she drove someone else's car that won't be connected back to her."

"It says here that ABLOY locks are used by the government and are made from boron-hardened steel."

"Fascinating." Michael glanced out the window again.

Olivia sat on the sofa and put her phone on the coffee table. "Michael, stop pacing. Kara's gonna be fine. She seems to have a good head on her shoulders, and she took a lot of precautions coming here."

"I hope you're right. If writing doesn't work out for me, maybe I could become a mortician."

Olivia frowned at him.

"Okay." He nodded, switching gears. "So that key most likely goes to a padlock?"

"That's what I'm guessing, but not just any padlock, these locks go for about two hundred dollars, so more like an industrial-strength lock."

"Unfortunately, that doesn't really help us. The match to this key could literally be anywhere in the world."

"You're right, but I had a thought," Olivia said, rising to her feet. "You said the woman looked at the envelope and then went ballistic because there was supposed to be a key inside, and it was missing."

"Yeah, and then she set fire to it." Michael opened his notepad to the last page. "I hid it in here."

He gently removed the charred envelope and placed it on the table.

"Why would she do that?" Olivia asked. "It doesn't make sense."

"Hmm, you're right again," Michael agreed. "Why didn't she just take it with her like the picture?"

"I'd burn it, if I didn't want anyone else to find it."

"True, but she took what was inside, the photo. The key was missing, so the envelope was no longer important to her."

"Then why go to the trouble of burning it, Michael?" She slid her finger across the screen of her phone and opened her camera app. "What if the place we're looking for was written on it?"

"You think that they would actually put the address on there?"

"There's no other reason to put a lighter to it."

"Maybe the envelope had some information hidden on it, and if she got caught, she didn't want it to fall into…."

"Michael," she said, leaning closer to her screen, moving her thumb and forefinger apart until the camera setting was at 5X magnification. "You're only proving my point. Most likely, something was written on the envelope, she memorized it and then set it on fire. Look," she said excitedly, "you can read the last few letters of the first two lines. Unfortunately, the rest is toast."

"There's a *phin,*" Michael said, "which we can guess is probably the tail end of the word dolphin, and the letters NC, for North Carolina. But for the rest…we'd need access to an FBI crime lab."

"Michael West," Olivia exclaimed, "you're brilliant! My brother attends Bramston Young University. Their chemistry program is one of the best in the nation."

"You think they're just going to let us waltz in there so we can analyze a charred envelope?"

"They will if they think they are assisting in an investigation, and our police department's forensic team is backed up for weeks."

"I see this ending badly." Michael moaned.

"Go change your clothes and make yourself presentable. I need to call Ellie and my brother."

Olivia was just ending the phone call with the words *I owe you big time* when Michael padded into the room. "My brother's going to hook us up with a friend who's majoring in biochemistry."

"You honestly think he's going to be able to recover anything from this?"

"Well, if you'd stop picking it up like that, maybe. Grab a freezer-sized Ziploc and a couple paper towels."

"Would you like some embalming fluids, too? I've got some out back, I keep them right next to my bone saw."

"You sure your thumb was the only thing that woman punched?"

"Here."

"Thank you." Olivia carefully sandwiched the envelope between the two paper towels and slid them into the freezer bag. She held the bag out and inspected her work. "Perfect."

Bramston Young University was a diamond in the rough. Nestled in the woodlands of North Carolina, an hour from Lana Cove, the campus was small but robust in regard to academia. Some of the nation's top professors had made Bramston their home. Giant red maples lined the entrance.

"This is gorgeous." Olivia laid her head back against the seat rest, watching the fiery-red blur of leaves pass over her.

Her brother told them to park and wait for him in front of the Copley Science building, located to the right off of the main entrance. He would provide them with VIP visitor cards and a day pass for their car.

"There's David." Olivia pointed to a tall, thin man in khakis and a white button-down dress shirt. He had the same rich, gold-colored hair as Olivia and identical striking cheekbones.

"There's no denying he's your brother," Michael observed.

David guided them into a visitor parking space and waved affectionately at Olivia. She jumped out of the car, ran to him, and wrapped her arms around him.

"Hey, sis, wonderful to see you!"

"You, too," she said brightly. "David," she turned toward Michael, "this is Michael."

"Nice to meet you." He shook David's hand. "Absolutely beautiful campus."

"It is, isn't it? So," he said, clasping his hands. "Livs tells me that you guys are in a bit of a hurry."

"We are, and I apologize for that. We've got some evidence that can't really wait to be processed through forensics. They have a major backlog—you know, all the bureaucratic red tape."

"I get it, especially with two murders in Lana Cove." He shook his head. "Insanity." David glanced at the Ziploc bag in Olivia's hand. "You know, sis, if you can't afford a purse, I could always lend you some money."

"Funny." She thumped him on the chest with her empty hand. "This is our properly secured evidence." She held up the plastic bag.

"Oh, yes, your charred remains." He grinned.

"We're hoping that your friend can work some magic and reveal the address."

"Let's get you in the lab. If anyone can turn back time, it's Abraham."

Dang, I was hoping he was going to say Cher.

"This is Copley Science Center," David said as they approached a big, rectangular, two-story building.

The front consisted of five massive sheets of glass that extended from floor to ceiling. The glass was framed in white and divided by six large columns. The walls were constructed of beautiful white sand-colored stones.

"How are classes going?" Olivia asked.

David led them down a wide hallway filled with numbered doors with tiny glass windows. "Wonderful. Kind of bummed that this is my last year."

"I get that." Olivia nodded.

"Hey, you're a big-time business owner. I hear that Bitter Sweet Café is really taking off. Let me know when you're ready to take your brand to the next level." He laughed, nudging her shoulder with his.

"David is a computer science genius," Olivia explained. "He thinks we should develop our own brand and create an online market."

"I agree with David, I think it's a great idea."

"And…here's the LCMS research facility." David came to a stop in front of a wooden door with a small rectangular glass window. He pressed the button below an intercom.

"What is LCMS?" Michael asked softly while they waited.

David shrugged. "I couldn't even begin to tell you."

"Abraham Leung, may I help you?" a soft voice said.

"Morning, Abraham, it's David Beckett."

There was a buzz, and then the metallic sound of an electric lock opening. A young Asian man with a boyish face and kind, intelligent brown eyes opened the door and greeted them.

"Abraham." David smiled, shaking his hand. "Good morning. Thank you so much for helping me out. This is my sister, Olivia."

Abraham looked from David to Olivia. "Uncanny. I recognize her from your pictures. Olivia, it's so nice to meet you." He stepped aside, motioning them into the lab. "David has told me so much about you. Congratulations on your new business venture."

"It's nice to meet you, and thank you so much." She punched her brother in the chest again. "Good job, little brother."

"And this is Michael." David appeared a little embarrassed. "I'm sorry, I don't know much about you."

"All the introduction I need." Michael smiled. He turned and shook Abraham's hand. "Thank you for working us into your schedule, we're on a bit of a time crunch with this one."

"I'm excited to help." Abraham rubbed his hands together. "Welcome to the Liquid Chromatography Mass Spectrometry research facility. All I ask is that you don't touch anything. You could be vaporized."

"I'm sure you just say that to impress the women." Michael smiled.

"Ah." Abraham laughed and shook a finger at Michael. "I like you already."

He led the group past rows of expensive-looking machines, racks of purple-capped test tubes, and computers, to a long table with a black rubber mat. "If I may, let's see what you've brought me."

Olivia unsealed the Ziploc and slid the paper towels to Abraham. He removed the top sheet and inspected the crispy envelope.

"I used to send my mail this way back in the late nineties. Hotmail." He laughed. "Get it? Remember the old email client?"

"That was good." Michael laughed, somewhat miffed that he hadn't come up with the joke first.

Abraham grabbed a shallow silver pan and, using forceps, he gently placed the envelope inside. "So, if we're lucky, whoever wrote the address used a ballpoint pen. Ballpoint pen ink contains trace amounts of metal, which are usually not destroyed by fire, especially something that would have burned at a low temperature intensity, like this."

"Have you done this type of…I don't even know what to call it," Olivia said. "Procedure? Test?"

"I'm a biochemistry major, but we were all required to take a semester of forensic science. We actually did an intensive lab on recovery of evidence damaged by fire, acid, and water." Abraham grabbed a spray bottle, shook it, and misted the envelope.

"I think it's a little late for sunscreen," Michael quipped.

"Aren't you the witty one," Abraham declared.

"Please don't encourage him," Olivia begged, "I have to drive back to Lana Cove with him."

"She's right," Michael said, "I'm incorrigible."

"What are you spraying on the envelope? It looks like it's some kind of oil?" Olivia asked.

"Brilliant observation." Abraham nodded. "It's a mixture of glycerin and water." He continued spraying until the envelope was completely saturated. "Now, if you'll excuse me for a second."

Abraham carried the tray to the other side of the lab and disappeared into a room simply marked IR. A few moments later, he returned with the tray. Behind them, a laser printer whirred to life.

"I used a powerful infrared camera to reveal what isn't visible to the naked eye. I think that you'll be pleasantly surprised by the results."

"You mean you did it?" Olivia had gone into this little adventure expecting the worst. She couldn't believe that it would actually be successful.

"See for yourself." He handed the image to Olivia.

Michael scooted around her to see. "I can't believe it. Abraham, no matter what anybody else says about you, I think you're a genius."

"Eh, it's pretty much what everybody thinks," Abraham confessed unabashedly.

The handwritten address seemed to float like white wispy clouds above the blackened surface of the envelope. "One hundred and three Blue Dolphin, Pelican Bay, NC three-three-two," Olivia read aloud. She slid her purse from her shoulder and grabbed her phone.

"If you're looking up the address," Abraham said, "it belongs to the Blue Coral Storage Facility. I searched for it while the print job was being sent to the laser printer," he added, nonchalantly.

"You're incredible," Olivia gushed.

"I excel at multi-tasking and prognostication."

"Careful," Michael joked, "I feel like you may be limiting yourself."

Abraham gently placed the envelope into a plastic bag and handed it to Olivia.

"Thank you again, Abe, you've been a tremendous help." She surprised him with a hug.

"Glad I could be of service." He blushed.

Olivia turned to her brother. Her face fell; she missed him. Between running the café with Ellie and his studies, it was rare that they got the opportunity to spend much time together.

"I know." David smiled sadly. "You've got to go. Come on, I'll walk you to your car."

The trio hurried through the halls of the science center. Olivia texted Ellie and gave her a brief overview of what had happened. She ended the text with: *I'll call you in a few.*

David collected their VIP IDs and then pulled his sister into his arms. "Next time, try and stay a little longer. I miss you."

"I will." She smiled. "I promise."

Chapter 11

Blue Coral Storage

Michael turned off River Road and took the on-ramp to the interstate, heading north. According to his GPS, Blue Coral Storage was about twenty minutes away.

"Okay, we'll see you there in a few," Olivia said, hanging up the phone.

"So, the plan is, Ellie is going to sign up for a storage unit, and then we'll do a little snooping?" Michael asked.

"Right. I don't think it's going to require too much snooping. I'm pretty sure the unit we're looking for is three-three-two."

"Or the beginning or ending of a zip code," Michael suggested. "It was right under the state."

"I thought of that, too; however, there aren't any zip codes in North Carolina that begin with three-three-two, and there are only two that end in three-

three-two, and they are at least a two-hour drive from here."

"I think your hunch is probably right," Michael agreed. "And if it's wrong, we'll just have to do a lot of walking."

"I still can't believe Abraham was able to recover the address."

Michael nodded. "Definitely impressive."

"What do you think's inside?"

"I don't know. Just as long as it's not another body. I've reached my quota. My next gig's going to require a black-hooded cloak and a scythe."

"I thought you were going to say priest, but grim reaper works, too." Olivia tapped her fingers on her phone. "Do you think we should call the police?"

Michael thought for a moment. "Not yet. I mean, honestly, what if it's nothing?"

"Yeah," Olivia agreed, "that would be a real bummer."

"We simply don't know. If Herb was hiding something, it could have been emptied out…. He's been dead for six months; they could have auctioned off whatever was inside."

"That's a lot of ifs. There's your exit, Blue Dolphin highway," Olivia said.

Michael eased his car onto the off ramp and merged onto Blue Dolphin highway, which was lined with upscale restaurants and exotic car dealerships.

"We're definitely in the right place." He glanced at the GPS. "Looks like it's just past that traffic light. There it is." He slowed and turned into the parking lot.

"There's Ellie's car; she beat us here. I'm surprised because she usually drives like an old lady."

"Nice place," he said as he pulled alongside Ellie's Acura.

"It should be." Olivia waved to Ellie. "According to their website, each unit is temperature-controlled, includes HEPA filtering, and can be video monitored from your home computer or cell phone using their app. All of this for the low, low cost of four hundred dollars a month."

"That's nearly five thousand a year! That's insane."

"Hey, guys," Ellie said, walking toward them, as they climbed out Michael's rental. "So we're renting a storage unit?"

"It seems that way." Olivia smiled. "I would tell them that we've acquired some high-end appliances for the new location, and we need some secure and clean place to store it."

"That's kind of along the same lines I was thinking. Livs, you're absolutely sure we can get out of the lease agreement as long as we cancel in seven days?"

"Positive, it's all over their website and posted in their legal disclaimer. This is a high-end facility, with nearly six hundred five-star reviews. I think we'll be okay," Olivia reassured her.

"Okay." Ellie sighed. "Let's do this."

"And simply sign here, and here." William, the office manager, pointed to the bottom of the contract where he'd attached a sticky note in the shape of a red arrow. He leaned back and pushed his glasses back up his nose.

Michael immediately loved him as a character for his book. His skin was white and blotchy with pink and brown patches. A face, Michael reasoned, was the result of someone who had neglected his skin for many years. His wispy hair was combed straight back and held in place by some type of gel that amassed here and there on his scalp like little beads of wax. His eyes, nose, and mouth were all tightly squeezed together on the front of a perfectly round head.

He wore an exceptionally tight, yellow, short-sleeved button-down that he tucked into a pair of khaki shorts, held up by a green-and-gold canvas belt. His sockless feet were squeezed into a pair of tasseled dress shoes.

While the man perused the contract, Michael slipped his phone out of his pocket, surreptitiously zoomed in on the man, and took a picture. *Click!* Michael's eyes bulged, and he fumbled with his phone, dropping it to the floor.

Olivia and Ellie spun in their seats, clearly mortified by his behavior.

"I'm so sorry," Michael said, picking up his phone. "I just wanted to capture this moment in a picture. I'm sure this happens all the time. I mean, this is the epitome of storage facility greatness."

The man's face transitioned from one of anger to one of pure delight. "Would you like to take another? How about me shaking her hand?"

"Uhm, yes, of course," Michael agreed.

"Ellie, if you could, turn your head a little so we can see your lovely profile," William suggested. He grasped her hand and swiveled toward the camera and smiled, revealing a mouth full of veneers.

"Perfect!" Michael exclaimed. "Perfect. What a gorgeous smile you have."

"If you don't mind," William requested, "if you'd please text me that photo, I'd love to have it."

"Of course, my pleasure," Michael said, as if there were no other option.

Ellie moved her head so William couldn't see her face and glared at Michael. She mouthed the word *payback* and then switched her attention back to William.

"Congratulations, Miss Banks." William beamed. "You are the proud owner of a Blue Coral Unit." He slid a black felt box across the table.

"I think he's proposing," Michael leaned forward, whispering into Olivia's ear.

"Thank you so much." Ellie reached for the box. "I'm so excited."

"As you should be. It's life-changing." He pushed his glasses back up his nose. "I never thought I would wish for a bigger nose, but once I hit forty, my vision started going, and now I've got to wear reading glasses. The struggles of everyday life."

"The struggle is real, my friend," Michael offered sagely.

"What does that even mean?" Olivia said under her breath.

The man nodded in agreement, picked up a metal pointer, and turned to a map of the facility. "Your new home is here." He tapped the map. "In building number two. Please observe the ten-mile-per-hour speed limit."

"Got it." Ellie clasped her hands together, anxious to leave. "Building two, obey the speed limit. Perfect."

Just as they were exiting, William called them back inside. "I'm so sorry, I must be getting rusty with age. I'm going to need at least one of you to stay and watch the orientation video. It's ten minutes, but I think it's a brilliant piece of cinematography."

Ellie surrendered the keys to Olivia, looking like a prisoner who had accepted their fate. "You guys go ahead. I'll watch the orientation video."

"Perfect," William said. "Follow me."

Ellie gave Olivia and Michael a *You owe me one* look as William led her into another room, talking about a local film crew and the aerial shots taken by a drone.

"I feel sorry for her," Olivia said once they were outside.

"But not so sorry you're willing to take her place?" Michael teased.

Olivia exhaled, avoiding his question. "That's ten minutes of her life she'll never get back."

"I know." Michael smiled evilly. "And I'm going to remind her of it over and over again."

Chapter 12

Hoodwinked

Michael drove up to the security gate and a phalanx of high-tech surveillance cameras. "Now what? Is there a keypad?"

"One second, I'm downloading the Blue Coral app."

"What happened to the good old days when you just had a clicker and you just point and click?"

"They're easily hacked; they're not secure at all."

"And your phone is?"

"Yep, each person is assigned an encrypted digital key. It generates a digital barcode which expires in sixty seconds. See?" Olivia held her screen so Michael could see. "Pull forward and hold the phone under that scanner."

"Cool, just like the airport," he said, laying her phone face down on the digital reader. He retrieved it as the gate rose. "I wonder how many people forget their phones."

"Probably a lot."

The Blue Coral Storage facility was made up of six massive concrete buildings. Michael guessed the width to be about that of a football field. A giant blue number was painted at the end of each building.

Both excitement and tension filled Olivia's body as Michael eased up to building three. *What if we're wrong? What if all of this has been a wild goose chase?*

Michael turned left, and she counted down the units.

"Three hundred and thirty, three hundred and thirty-one, three hundred and thirty-two," she exclaimed.

Each storage unit looked like a condo, complete with a regular and a garage-style door.

"There's the lock!" Olivia said, excited.

Michael had barely stopped the car before she was out the door and running.

Michael, pushed the door open with his knee, and stole a glance over his shoulder. "There're cameras on each corner of this building," he cautioned. "Not sure how long we're gonna have before security arrives to check us out." He pulled out his wallet—he'd hidden the key behind his driver's license so he wouldn't lose it. He slid the key into the lock and twisted. It sprang open.

Michael paused in the doorway, letting his eyes adjust to the dim light. The HEPA filters had done their job—the air was crisp, cool, and clean. He stepped aside, and Olivia entered behind him. The storage unit was completely empty except for an old blanket.

"Well," Olivia said, "that's kind of disappointing."

"What did you expect? King Tut's tomb?"

"Well, a little more than this." She spread out her hands.

Michael strode to the back and gently lifted the blanket. "Please don't be a body, please don't be a body."

"What is it?" Olivia's shoulder brushed his.

"I'm not sure, I think Herb must have been a minimalist."

There were two boxes stacked on top of each other, about the size of a muffin tin, with a smaller one, the size of a cigarette pack, placed on the floor beside them.

Michael crouched and gently lifted the first one. It weighed less than a pound. He fished his keys out of his pocket and, using the rough edge, pulled the teeth along the tape that secured the box. "Nuts," he said softly.

"Nuts?" Olivia asked, confused.

"Packaging peanuts." He removed the Styrofoam peanuts by hand, revealing yet another box. He grabbed his keys, gently cut through the tape, and pulled open the top. "It's a painting, I can see the frame, but it's secured in…." He tugged on the frame. "It looks like it's sealed in an airtight plastic bag."

"A painting? Can you tell what it is?"

"No, it's wrapped in so much plastic—but if someone went to this much trouble…it's probably worth a fortune." He gently lowered the painting back inside the box.

"Valuable enough to kill over. I'm guessing the other one is going to be a painting, too."

"Most likely," Michael agreed. He picked up the smaller one. It felt like a brick. He sliced through the tape and folded the flaps back. "It's glass. Liv, hold out your hands. It's heavy, so be careful."

Olivia placed her hands together, and Michael gently shook the contents into her palms. Two thick pieces of glass encased a postage stamp.

"A stamp," Olivia whispered. "I guess it's super valuable?"

"Probably so, it's printed upside down, so most likely a mistake."

"That's right," a man said behind them.

Olivia jumped and nearly sent the glass box flying.

"Careful with that, it's a misprint from nineteen-eighteen, and it's worth one and a half million dollars."

"Maxwell…Kara?" Michael gawped at them, confused. "What are you doing here? How did you get here?"

"Michael, you look so confused. Your dear friend Ellie helped us get through the gate. Such a sweet girl."

"Yep, seemed my cell phone couldn't get a signal again." Kara smiled mockingly.

"Where's Ellie? You didn't hurt Ellie, did you?"

"Lands no, boy. What kind of monster do you take me for? She's off to meet you guys at your new unit. That's why we need to hurry."

"Wait, how did you find us? How did you know we were here?"

"Let's just say that you should be a little more careful with who you let use your phone."

Olivia stared at Michael. "She used your phone?"

"She said she didn't have a signal. How was I supposed to know she was lying?"

"All right, enough with all the chit-chat. My beautiful wife and I are here to simply collect what is rightfully ours, and then we'll be on our way."

"Wife? Yours?" Michael wasn't sure which surprised him the most. "This isn't yours."

"It certainly is. This was a part of Herb's property when we originally secured the house. Herb put me in charge of negotiating the sale of all of his property—that included furniture, his car, and any valuables. Which I must say," he laughed, "is *extremely* valuable."

Olivia glared at them. "And now that he's conveniently dead, you think that you're entitled to all of his belongings? You're evil, Maxwell, pure evil."

"I told you he was." Kara laughed. "You should have listened." She turned to Michael and smiled. "No hard feelings, I hope?"

Anger tore through Michael's veins. "So what? Did you kill Herb? Did you orchestrate this whole thing so you could take his house and his money? And you used us to find…."

"I guess you'll never know, will you?" Maxwell interrupted.

"And now what, are you going to kill me and Olivia, too? There're cameras everywhere, you'd never get away with it."

"Why would I? I've done nothing wrong. And no one can prove or disprove that I killed Herb."

"I'm going to call the police," Olivia said defiantly. "We're not going to let you simply waltz in here and take everything. This is something for the police to handle."

"I don't think so," another voice said.

This time it was Maxwell's and Kara's turn to be surprised. A petite man with bleach-blond hair and sunglasses stood in the doorway, a pistol in his hand.

"Who in tarnation are you?"

"Shut up, Maxwell, or that pretty wife of yours is going to be a widow."

Maxwell clenched his fist. Michael thought he was going to argue back, but then he decided against it.

"Now, this is going to go down nice and easy. Everyone's phones on the floor." He slowly moved his gun from person to person. "Good. Now kick them to me."

Each person kicked their phone, sending them skittering across the floor. Keeping an eye on his captives, he slid the phones out the door.

"That was easy." He grinned. "It's so nice when we all work together. Whose BMW?"

"Mine," Michael said. "You can have it, it's a rental, full tank of gas." He tossed the keys to the man who left them lying at his feet.

"You," he said, pointing the gun at Michael, "bring me those boxes, and hurry."

Michael stacked the boxes on top of each other, crouched, and picked them up.

"Put them in the trunk of the car. Any funny business, and I'll kill your friends."

Michael nodded. "That won't be necessary. I'll do what you tell me." His eyes caught Olivia's. "We'll get out of this," he whispered.

"Shut up," the man screamed.

He backed out of the storage unit and waited for Michael to emerge. As soon as Michael stepped outside, he turned and slammed the door, locking Max, Kara, and Olivia in the storage unit.

"Well, that was remarkably easy." He smiled.

"Now that you've got what you want, why not just leave?"

"Oh no, no, no. Not until I'm safely up in the air, and far away from here."

"Then why do you need me? I'll keep my mouth shut for hours, until you're out of the country, or wherever you plan on going."

The man sneered at Michael and swung his pistol, catching him just below the ear. Michael staggered and fell hard against his car. Stars exploded in his head. He climbed up onto the trunk, trying not to black out.

"Now do you understand how serious I am? Get in the car, you're driving."

Michael's head felt like it was going to burst. *The idiot hits me in the head, and now he wants me to drive?* He made his way around to the driver's side and slid into the front seat. The gunman climbed in beside him. He held the gun in his right hand, across his body.

Chapter 13

A Daring Escape

"Drive!" the man ordered.

Michael stared straight ahead. He put the car in gear, drove to the end of the lot, and made a left in front of building two. *Oh no, there's Ellie's car. If he sees her....*

Michael turned toward the man and pointed at the GPS in an attempt to distract him. "Do you want me to punch in the address?"

The ruse worked. The man glanced at the GPS just as they passed Ellie's silver Acura.

"No," the man answered sharply. "I know where we're going."

Michael pulled through the gate. A golf cart marked 'security' whizzed past them.

The gunman twisted in his seat. "Too late!" He laughed. "Go!"

"Which way? Right? Left?"

"Left, left." The man slammed his hand on the dash. "Go!"

Michael whipped the car onto Blue Dolphin highway, heading south. Behind them, William rushed out onto the sidewalk in front of his office, his phone in his hand.

"Stay calm and do exactly what I tell you, and you might make it through this alive."

Michael didn't reply. He didn't want to do anything to trigger the man.

"Stay on this road for two miles. Don't speed, don't do anything stupid to draw attention, or I'll put a bullet in that knee, got it?"

Michael nodded this time and immediately regretted it. His head was pounding. In the distance, he thought he heard the faint wail of a siren. His captor heard it, too; he checked the side mirror.

"Step on it!"

"But you said—"

The man raised the gun as if he was going to strike Michael again.

"Sorry!" Michael shouted, throwing up his hand to protect his head. "I'm speeding, I'm speeding," he cried.

The highway opened up to two lanes, and Michael gunned the engine.

"In about half a mile, you're gonna turn right on Airport Lane."

"We're going to the airport?"

"What, did you think I was gonna drive out of the country? Of all the people, I pick an idiot."

A powerful engine revved behind them. Michael glanced at the rearview mirror. A black Ford Mustang pulled up beside them, blue lights flashing in its grill.

"Pull over!" the officer yelled.

The man shoved his gun against Michael's head and screamed, "Back off, or I swear I'll kill him!"

The police officer immediately pumped his brakes and fell behind their car. Michael saw another police car, flying over the hill toward them. This wasn't going to end well.

"What do you want me to do?"

"Keep driving, you idiot."

"They'll arrest us at the airport. They'll never let us board a plane."

"It's a private airport, we'll drive straight to the terminal. They won't shoot." He smiled. "Because I'm going to use you as my human shield."

"Glad to hear I'm useful."

The man turned and grinned evilly. It was just the opportunity Michael had been waiting for. He jerked the car hard to the right, slamming the passenger's side into a telephone pole.

Everything happened at once. The scraping sound of metal, the jarring impact, the explosion of the airbags driving them back into their seats, the car spinning like a top. Michael hit the release on his seat belt, knocked his door open with his shoulder, fell hard to the ground, and ran.

He didn't turn to see if the man had survived the crash. He bolted toward a large concrete storm drain, filled waist deep with water. He'd just leaped in when a piece of concrete the size of his fist exploded inches away from his head, sending debris into his face.

"I'm going to kill you!" the man screamed.

Michael dove into the water, willing himself to move forward into the culvert that ran beneath the highway. Suddenly his back arched violently, he sucked in a lungful of water, and a blinding pain tore through his shoulder. *This is it*. Michael convulsed, choking on the water. He thought of his daughter, and Ellie, sweet Ellie. *Goodbye*, he exhaled, and the world went black.

Chapter 14

A Second Chance

"Welcome back to the land of the living."

Michael's eyes slowly focused. He recognized that voice. His lips felt so strange, so dry.

"Detective Adams? Where am I?" he whispered.

"Saint Mary's Hospital," Ellie said, holding his hand. Her eyes were swollen.

Michael could tell she'd been crying.

"Everyone is okay?" he asked.

"Everyone's fine." Ellie nodded. "Well, except for you." She rubbed the back of his hand. "You're a little banged up, but they tell me you're going to live."

"And what about the man, the man who kidnapped me?"

"Herb Beaumont." Detective Adams shook his head. "I'm sad to say he didn't make it."

"Did someone give me too much morphine? Did you say Herb Beaumont?" Michael moaned and closed his eyes.

"Yes, in disguise."

"Then who was that in my backyard? I thought that was Herb."

"Rupert, Herb's twin brother," Detective Adams explained.

"Herb and Rupert. Surprised they didn't kill their parents for giving them those names." Michael smiled wanly. "So, does this mean, I lose the house?"

"Well, being that Herb was still alive, and according to Maxwell King, all of the documentation and paperwork for the sale of the home was legal...," Detective Adams shrugged his shoulders, "as far as we're concerned—and Judge Morris is concerned—you own the house."

Michael exhaled, a look of relief flooded his face. "Thank you," he said softly, "I needed that."

"Michael," Olivia interrupted, "you're exhausted. We can catch you up on all of this once you're up to it. Right now, you need to rest."

"Okay," Michael agreed, "but wait, just one more question. Why did Herb kill his brother?"

"Remember the woman who was killed?" asked Detective Adams.

"Yes, of course," Michael said. "I've been shot, I don't have amnesia. Wait, do I?"

"You've got something a little more special than that." Ellie winked and squeezed his hand.

"Michael," Detective Adams continued, "we found a picture in the woman's jacket. She was in the photo, Herb and Rupert were in the photo, and then one other person, but there was substantial water damage done to it, so we can't identify the fourth person."

"Maybe Abraham can help."

"I'll explain later," Olivia said, gesturing for him to keep going.

"What we do know, is that this group was involved in a series of robberies throughout Europe. It seems that Herb skipped out on them and disappeared with a lot of cash, a series of paintings valued in the millions and, as you discovered, a rare stamp."

"I feel like there's so much more." Michael moaned again.

"Yes, there is. I'm sure my niece will fill you in with all the details when you're better."

"Niece? Olivia? I seem to be hallucinating." Confusion filled Michael's face.

"I'm sorry, Michael." Olivia smiled gently. "I couldn't say anything to you. I wanted to, but if it makes you feel any better, I did make him pinky promise not to go too hard on you."

"She did say to keep an eye on you. Something about, if you died you wouldn't be able to finish your novel, and she's counting on the royalties to finish her master's."

"Your niece." Michael closed his eyes. "This is all a dream," he whispered.

"Okay." Detective Adams smiled. "I guess that's my cue. You did a great job, Michael, I'm proud of you. Just one thing, if I may. Next time I tell you to call me, if you find something, do me a favor, and make the call."

"Agreed." Michael gave him a thumbs-up. "Oh, they fixed my thumb!" he exclaimed, noticing the metal splint and gauze for the first time.

"They took care of that while you were under," Olivia explained.

Michael looked at his two friends. Even with a bullet in his shoulder and bandages covering his face, he still felt like he was the luckiest man alive.

"We're going to get going, Michael. Visiting hours are over, and the floor nurse has glared at me a dozen times." Ellie leaned over and tenderly kissed him on his cheek, brushing stray hairs from his forehead.

"Thank you, Ellie, for everything."

"I'll come by and check on you tomorrow. Get some rest."

Olivia rose off her heels and kissed him, then playfully touched his nose. Her eyes slid from his to the cup of green Jell-O on his bedtime table, which he'd been looking forward to eating as soon as they left.

"Green Jell-O!" Olivia gasped. "Do you know how long it's been?"

"Take it." Michael laughed. "I wasn't going to eat it anyways."

More from T. Lockhaven

We hope you enjoyed reading *A Garden to Die For*, the first book in *The Coffee House Sleuths*!

Also written in the series is *Sleighed*, the first book in *The Coffee House Sleuths: A Christmas Cozy Mystery*. *Sleighed* takes place in the same town, with the same characters, but was written as a fun standalone Christmas story. You may find the paperback version on Amazon and Barnes & Noble.

Sign up for the latest info on book releases and bonus content at twistedkeypublishing.com

Let us know what you think by leaving a review on Amazon, Barnes & Noble and/or Goodreads. Thank you so very much!

T. Lockhaven is also a children's author under the name Thomas Lockhaven.

Ava & Carol Detective Agency Series
Book 1: The Mystery of the Pharaoh's Diamonds
Book 2: The Mystery of Solomon's Ring
Book 3: The Haunted Mansion
Book 4: Dognapped
Book 5: The Eye of God
Book 6: The Crown Jewels Mystery
Book 7: The Curse of the Red Devil (Upcoming title)

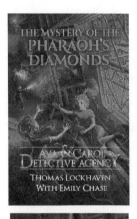

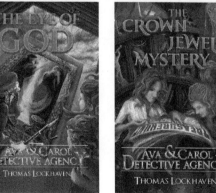

Quest Chasers series
Book 1: The Deadly Cavern
Book 2: The Screaming Mummy

The Ghosts of Ian Stanley series

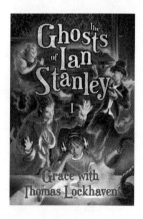

Learn about new book releases by signing up at twistedkeypublishing.com. You may also learn of new releases by following T. Lockhaven's author page on Amazon or on Bookbub and hitting the +Follow button.

Made in the USA
Middletown, DE
11 December 2020